BREATH BY BREATH

By Morgan Llywelyn from Tom Doherty Associates

MORGAN LLYWELYN

BREATH BY BREATH

TOR

A TOM DOHERTY ASSOCIATES BOOK

NEW YORK

BREATH BY BREATH

Copyright © 2021 by Morgan Llywelyn

A Tor Book
Published by Tom Doherty Associates
120 Broadway
New York, NY 10271

www.tor-forge.com

Tor® is a registered trademark of Macmillan Publishing Group, LLC.

The Library of Congress Cataloging-in-Publication Data is available upon request.

ISBN 978-0-7653-8872-8 (hardcover)
ISBN 978-0-7653-8874-2 (ebook)

Our books may be purchased in bulk for promotional, educational, or business use. Please contact your local bookseller or the Macmillan Corporate and Premium Sales Department at 1-800-221-7945, extension 5442, or by email at MacmillanSpecialMarkets@macmillan.com.

First Edition: April 2021

Printed in the United States of America

0 9 8 7 6 5 4 3 2 1

For Sean, Holly, and
Micaela
The clan

BREATH BY BREATH

1

As the double doors slid open the people inside the barn waited, eager yet fearful to see what the daylight would reveal. They had spent months underground waiting for this moment. The fecund smell of the earth still coated the insides of their nostrils.

They hungrily gulped their first breaths from the outside world.

Hot summer air scorched their throats.

Bathed in buttery light, a hilly, sun-parched pasture sloped down toward a rambling white farmhouse built for a large family and encircled by a rail fence. Beside the front gate an unobtrusive sign identified the property as TILBURY FARM.

Close to the back of the house was a kitchen garden. Parallel rows of dry, cracked earth testified to the onions, carrots and lettuce, the tomatoes and cabbage and bush beans that once flourished there. Gone now; all that remained were a few dying weeds, the stubborn survivors of months without rain. At one end of the garden dead raspberry canes drooped from a wooden lattice. Beyond this was a small orchard of apple and pear trees, with a few brown leaves clinging to otherwise bare branches.

There was little sign of life. No birds were declaring their territory with song. The cacophony of insects that should accompany a summer morning in the country was curiously muted.

Edgar Tilbury shook his grizzled head. Guessing his age would be difficult; it might be anywhere between sixty and eighty. Below tangled eyebrows were sharp features and bright eyes that revealed a keen intelligence. "There you have it," he growled in a voice like a rusty hinge. "My first wife and I planted that garden; I've tended it all these years since she died, though I never had her green thumb. It was that produce we lived on underground, but it looks like global warming's finished it off now. If that wasn't bad enough, the land may have taken a dose of radiation too. Damn all the megalomaniacs and their pissing contests. This time the whole world lost."

A three-legged Rottweiler bumped its muzzle against his thigh, seeking attention. Edgar reached down to rumple the animal's ears. "Don't worry, Samson," he told the dog. "You're not to blame, humans cause all the trouble."

"Amen to that," agreed Jack Reece. A tall, lean man with dark hair and a hawkish nose, he possessed a sinewy strength. Smile lines bracketed his pale gray eyes but he was not smiling now. "We won't know how bad things are until we do some investigating."

"Can't you feel it in your bones, Jack? I damn sure can. The war's come and gone and we're all that's left. What's happened to the birds and the butterflies? You can't tell me another damned heat wave carried them off."

A small blond woman laid a supplicating hand on Tilbury's arm. "Edgar, you assured us there would be plenty of other survivors."

"There will be, Nell." He tried to sound more convinced than he felt. "Everybody's not dead, we'll find them soon enough. Or they'll find us. It's just that things seem different now; even the light looks different. Yellower; meaner."

"Don't let your imagination run away with you," Jack said. "There's been a drought, that's all; there's nothing mean about sunshine. Never bleed before you're wounded, that's my motto. C'mon, let's see if there's been any damage around here and look for something to eat. Tomorrow we can go to Sycamore River and find out what it's like over there. It may not be as bad as we think." He squared his shoulders and stepped into the sunlight. A dozen people, several dogs and a small troop of cats followed him.

They saw no visible danger.

The invisible threat was terrifying.

Edgar Tilbury's wife used her forefinger to adjust the gold frames of her spectacles on the bridge of her nose. Before her marriage she had been Beatrice Fontaine, chief officer in the Sycamore and Staunton Mercantile Bank. An air of authority had been necessary for the job and the spectacles were part of that image, augmented by her silver hair and ramrod spine.

"You children stay in the barn until we decide it's safe to come out," she called over her shoulder.

A youthful protest—it might be either Flub or Dub, the twins' voices were as identical as their faces—retorted, "We're not kids, we're breeding age!"

"Since when did pubescent mean breeding age?" Gerry Delmonico muttered to his wife.

Gloria looked up at him. "Philip and Daniel may be smart-alecks, but they'll do what they're told. I don't want to bring any of our family outside until we're sure." Since adopting the twins she had been trying without success to establish the use of their proper names. Even her husband resisted, though he adored his wife and gave way to her in most things.

After a decade of marriage the handsome black couple still held hands.

Walking behind them, Lila Ragland remarked to Shay Mulligan, "This must be what it was like to come off Noah's Ark two by two."

Shay, who had never outgrown the freckles that accompanied his red hair, said, "You suppose Noah had a doctor on board?"

"Not one as good as you."

"I'm just a small town veterinarian. I hope I won't have to take care of elephants and ostriches; we didn't study exotics at the college I went to."

"If any 'exotics' did survive there may be some strange mutations among them. They'd appear fairly soon too. Other animals have a shorter lifespan than we do."

"Tell me something I don't know."

"None of us know what we're facing," Lila responded. "We can't even be sure we'll survive today."

Shay's son, Evan, followed them from the barn. Taller than his father, he was a lithe young man with a mop of red-gold hair and gentle brown eyes. Before he stepped into the sunlight he glanced back, looking for Jessamyn Bennett.

He found her sitting cross-legged on a bale of straw amid a clutter of farm machinery. A willowy girl in faded blue jeans, with a cotton shirt knotted beneath her small breasts, Jess wore her curly hair pulled into a ponytail. While Evan watched, she wiped the perspiration from her forehead with the back of her wrist.

Just seeing her made Evan feel warm inside.

As far as he was concerned, there was no comparison between Jess and Lila Ragland. Lila was ancient by his standards, late thirties at least, with slanted green eyes and a heavy mane of auburn hair. Men like his father turned to look at her in the street but she did not appeal to Evan. When he dreamed it was always of Jess.

One of his favorite fantasies involved a picnic where they spread a blanket on the ground and she sat with his head pillowed in her lap, smiling fondly down at him while she stroked his hair.

In Evan's dream two moons were in the sky above them, Phobos and Deimos; the moons that beamed down on Mars Settlement.

At the moment, Jess Bennett's lap was occupied by a massive black cat named Karma. The cat had been a gift to Shay from Lila. The Bennett family's Irish setters, Sheila and Shamrock—who was affectionately known as Rocky—lay at her feet, only pretending to be relaxed; they were keenly aware of the cat's presence. The dogs had had no experience of cats until they had found themselves in an underground bomb shelter with Beatrice Fontaine's seven felines. Their period of adjustment in the subterranean labyrinth Edgar called his "bolt-hole" had not been easy.

Karma was well acquainted with dogs; Samson was an old friend from the time they had spent together in Shay's vet clinic. The black cat was fearsomely armed with fang and claw. No mere canine could intimidate her, a fact she had amply demonstrated to the setters on more than one occasion. Jess had been given the job of keeping the potential combatants apart.

When she felt the weight of Evan's gaze, the girl smoothed her hair with the palm of her hand.

Kirby, at nineteen the oldest of the Delmonicos' four adopted sons, was the last to leave the barn. He also glanced back toward Jess, then hastily turned away. Those who had been with him in the shelter were used to his appearance, but he still tried to shield them from the sight of his disfigurement. Severe phosphorous burns had scarred the left half of his face and pulled that side of his mouth into a rictus grin. At the time of the accident he had raised his hands to protect his face, otherwise it might have been worse. But although he could use them, both hands were twisted into claws. His speech had been slightly affected by his injury, resulting in a faint sibilance when he was excited; another handicap he struggled to overcome.

There had been discussion of plastic surgery to repair the damage done when Robert Bennett's factory exploded, but the onset of war had intervened.

Jess was the person whose opinion Kirby cared about most. He could never tell her that. In his heart he saw himself as a monster.

"You think it'd be okay to let the horses out to graze?" Evan was asking Edgar. "They've been living on dry straw for weeks and they've lost a lot of condition."

"There's not much nourishment left in that dead grass, but there could be some radiation. We'll know soon. Those four horses are our only reliable transportation, we can't afford to take chances with them."

Evan was indignant. "I'd never take chances with Rocket!"

"You almost rode her to Nolan's Falls and got caught up in the bombing," Edgar reminded him. "Shay, you have that Geiger counter ready?"

"Right here."

"Turn it on, then, You go down the left side of the hill and I'll take the other side. Walk slow, do it like a grid. The rest of you hold back until we get to the bottom and have a definitive reading." He turned a knob on his own counter.

The machine responded with the kind of faint, chitinous clicking that might come from an insect; an insect with a venomous bite.

"Does that mean . . ."

"It doesn't mean anything, Nell, it's natural background radiation. Long as it's no louder than that we're all right."

"What if your counter's wrong?"

"That's why I have two counters, I'm a natural-born belt-and-suspenders man. Both counters wouldn't fail; in fact the signal's fading now. Looks like it'll be safe to use my house. If you want to, you're all welcome to stay there until we find out what's happened to your own homes. Bea and I will do our best to make you comfortable. After all those weeks underground you must be sick of living in tunnels."

"At least it was cool down there," said Nell. "I'll always be grateful you shared the shelter with us; you saved our lives."

Edgar gave a negligible shrug, as if it was nothing at all.

Like children following the Pied Piper, the little group picked its way down the slope of the hill. The footing was uncertain, hummocky in some places and rocky in others.

Gloria Delmonico paused to untie the laces of her sandals and remove them. Knotting the laces together, she hung them from the leather belt around her waist. "I love walking barefoot on the grass."

"It's safe enough," Shay assured her. "I'm not getting a dangerous reading."

"Watch where you're walking, though," Evan called. "There

are a few dead birds lying on the ground, I almost stepped on one."

"Today's going to be another scorcher," Gerry predicted as he rolled up his sleeves.

Nell agreed. "The air's awfully heavy. I hate hot weather. Has it always been this hot in the summer?"

"Not always; according to the met office our weather's been getting more extreme year by year," said Gerry. "We've been having hotter summers, colder winters, more frequent storms and worse floods. Hurricane and tornado season start earlier too, and last longer . . . not to mention the increase in volcanic and seismic activity since the last century."

"The air smells odd to me," Lila remarked. "Not really clean . . . but sharp."

Jack lifted a single eyebrow. "What did you expect?"

"After a nuclear war? Radioactive clouds, I suppose."

Jack shook his head. "Nothing may be the way we thought it would be, we'll have to take it as it comes. Keep your expectations low. We're alive; everything else is a bonus."

At the foot of the hill the two-storey farmhouse was waiting for them. Untouched by destruction, it still had walls to embrace a family and a roof to shelter them. Windows to let in the daylight; shutters to keep out the night.

A house designed for normal life in a normal world.

Home.

The word had a special meaning for every person in the group. Home might be a new house in a leafy suburb, with a bicycle lying beside the driveway, or the residence of grandparents in a long-established neighborhood, where a lawnmower awaited use on the weekends. It could summon a mental image of a modern apartment or an old-fashioned boarding house.

Home was where you could shut the door and leave the world outside.

The little group stood silent for a moment, as if in homage.

"Looks like there's no harm done," Edgar said with relief. "When I bought this place I got fifteen acres including the house and barn, and I'd damned sure hate to lose any of it. We may need this farm to support us for a while, so it's a good thing we have the garden and a woodlot. Any of you know if we can restore the vegetable garden?"

Gerry said, "My wife can make anything grow, she even talks to her plants."

Laughing, Gloria gave him a gentle punch on the arm. "I do not."

But she did.

In keeping with rural custom the house faced the road to town, rather than the barn on the hill. The foundation was concealed by shrubbery wilting in the heat. A flat-roofed back porch shaded the kitchen door and the downstairs windows from the summer sun. The porch, which ran the width of the house, was furnished with an old rocking chair and an assortment of wicker armchairs.

Gerry bounded up the steps. "My grandmother used to have chairs just like these!"

Edgar stopped him with an upraised hand. "Don't sit on one until I get a reading."

"You have to measure everything first? I doubt if the . . ."

"We can't be too careful, Gerry. Being bombarded by radioactive particles can break your DNA apart."

"The war ended months ago."

"That wouldn't matter to residual radioactivity. And I don't think you can say it 'ended.' Both sides agreed to an armistice, but that's only another word for truce, not a binding declaration of peace. Words matter. Truce means 'we'll hold our fire until we have a better chance of winning.' There was an armistice at the end of the First World War; the one they called 'The War To End All Wars.' It wasn't worth the paper it was printed on, and neither is the current truce. The damage is ongoing because the half-life of . . ."

"Don't give me a lecture on the effects of radiation, Edgar. We've had time to learn more about that than we ever wanted to know. We can't do anything about the situation but adjust to it as best we can, and hope evolution will take care of future human generations, if any."

"If any," Edgar echoed. He did not sound hopeful.

One of the Irish setters scratched on the screen door, seeking admittance.

The screen door was not latched but the door behind it was closed. Jack jiggled the handle. "It's not locked."

"We never locked our doors," said Edgar. "Never needed to, that's one of the things Veronica and I liked about living out in the country." He gave a deep sigh. "Come on in."

Kirby said to Bea, "I heard him mention Veronica when we were in the shelter. Who was she?"

"She was his first wife; her name was Mary Veronica Tilbury but he just called her Veronica. She died a dozen years ago."

"Oh. I'm sorry."

"Edgar was too. He sold his engineering firm; it was almost like he gave up on life for a while." Bea gave a tiny smile. "He's better now, though."

Veronica had been gone for a long time yet her touch remained; she had turned a large but basic farmhouse into an elegant rural retreat. The kitchen was fully equipped with urban conveniences but its waxed pine paneling evoked the countryside. A swinging door gave access to a formal dining room; beyond that was an inviting living room papered in a sophisticated blue-and-white-striped pattern. The soft furnishings were deeply upholstered in Williamsburg blue; the huge fireplace could have held a roast ox. The floor was carpeted wall to wall in pearl gray wool. From the raftered ceiling hung a perfectly scaled bronze and crystal chandelier. Empty bookshelves gave mute testimony to a large personal library that had been relocated elsewhere. A well-worn recliner upholstered in copper-colored velour stood beside a large floor lamp. In the center of the room was a low glass table with chairs on either side. The table held an assortment of dusty magazines ranging from *Vogue* and *Architectural Digest* to *Engineering Today*.

Edgar extended his Geiger counter and cocked his head while he listened. "It's okay, safe enough. We could make this a staging area. What do you think, Jack?"

Edgar Tilbury was a generation older than Jack Reece, yet during their time in the bomb shelter the unsought mantle of leadership had settled on the younger man. In a crisis Jack was calm and steady, inclined to think before he acted. He was thorough about whatever he did. He never ignored a fact but simply filed it away—nothing was trivial. His memory was not photographic but it was inclusive, and his curiosity extended to a wide variety of subjects. "Jack of all trades, master of none," was how his Aunt Bea described him; she did not necessarily mean it as a compliment. He was an adventurer by nature and his inability to settle down had been a sore point between them.

Before Nell.

Jack had enjoyed many women but never thought he was an emotional man. He could not explain his feelings for Nell. He only knew that her skin felt right and her hair smelled right; the sound of her voice resonated in his bones. When she touched him a spark leaped between them that he had never experienced before.

As a test for the limits of his courage, occasionally Jack tried to imagine what he would do if anything happened to Nell. He always lost his nerve at the last moment. Without her there would be, could be, nothing. He did not tell her this; his vulnerabilities he kept to himself.

Others saw only the image Jack chose to project: his public face. Thinking he understood the man, Edgar said of him, "Jack's a natural leader, folks follow him the way metal filings gravitate to a magnet."

"I agree about the staging area," Jack told Edgar now. "We should start bringing things up from the shelter. One item we're going to need right away is your industrial generator. The air's cool enough down below, but in this weather we'll be thankful for that big fridge-freezer in your kitchen."

"What do we have that's going to need chilling?"

"Nothing right now, but we will," Jack said. "We might even find a few vegetables hidden among the weeds in your garden. We'll keep using our oil lamps so we can conserve fuel for the generator until we locate a source for more. And we have candles, there are boxes of them left. My wife thinks candlelight's more romantic anyway.

"We'll bring the candles along with anything else we might need right away. We'll load up the horse-bus with enough for a couple of weeks; no more until we have a better idea of how things are. And be sure to check them with one of the Geiger counters before we carry them into the house. How many bedrooms do you have here, Edgar?"

"One downstairs and three upstairs, plus what we called 'the spare room' because we dumped everything into it. There's a foldaway bed in the cedar closet on the landing too. We wanted to be prepared for guests but we didn't encourage any; we were happy just being with each other. We can put pallets on the floor if need be; it'll be a lot better than huddling underground, waiting for World War Three."

They knew what it was like to wait for World War Three; to expect death to come winging toward you at any moment and know you were helpless. Ordinary, everyday life had once seemed like the norm. Circumstances had proved it was the brink of an abyss. A word, a smell, a casual reference were enough to bring the darkness flooding back.

A sudden thud overhead startled Nell. Invisible pins and needles pricked her skin. "Is someone else here, Edgar?"

"A ghost, maybe?" Kirby suggested.

At his words Bea glimpsed a brief flicker of excitement in her husband's eyes. She and Edgar had not been married long, but it was long enough for her to realize there were three in the marriage. Bea knew a woman in her sixties could never compete with a girl who had died at the height of her youth and beauty.

Veronica was a perfect butterfly held in the amber of Edgar Tilbury's memory.

"I'll go up and see what's what." Jack took the carpeted steps two at a time and disappeared beyond the turn of the landing. Edgar followed him. Samson started to go after them but changed his mind.

The Rottweiler sat down on his haunches at the foot of the stairs and whined.

2

By the standards of war, Sycamore River and Nolan's Falls should have gotten off lightly. The medium-sized town of Sycamore River was set in a location of natural beauty between a river and a forest. It might almost have been Greenfield Village, the tribute to nostalgia that Henry Ford had constructed in the previous century as a fantasy of the childhood he never had. For generations Sycamore River had conformed to its own rhythms. Youngsters who grew up there might move away, but they usually came back to retire. Those who could not afford to travel abroad bought motor homes and set off to tour America. They sent back scenic postcards to the folks at home.

Nolan's Falls was an unprepossessing small city relying on its own local commerce and service industries. It owed its name to a waterfall that had been destroyed in the seventeenth century when Nolan Ryder dammed the creek for his mill.

Nolan's Falls was resolutely middle class, with a middle-class outlook. When one of its inhabitants was elected to the state senate, he had campaigned hard for a hyperloop between his hometown and the capital, to cut travel time for his staffers who had to make the journey twice a day, and wanted expense money for it. The fledgling senator served only one term before the voters rejected him for someone younger and more telegenic, who had promised them a municipal swimming pool.

For decades both communities had been struggling with the effects of climate change as wave after wave of searing heat swept the planet. Nearing the end of the twenty-first century portions of Africa and Asia and even some parts of southern Europe were no longer habitable. It was popular to blame the weather for everything—especially the threat of war.

Before the first bombs fell, civic authorities had assumed that neither town offered a target sufficient to justify an attack. Sycamore River had been a railway hub before the failure of metal alloys crippled the railroads. The factories in Nolan's Falls concentrated on building wooden furniture and manufacturing glass bottles. The area between the two was devoted to agriculture. Fields and pastures were not worth an expenditure of bombs and missiles . . . unless mindless destruction was the ultimate goal.

Which it was.

The first wave of attack had come up from the south—no one had expected a nuclear attack from the south—and devastated great swaths of the countryside.

The damage to the United States as a whole was still too large to calculate, but every change of the wind carried a fresh veil of dust containing the pulverized atoms of the land of the free and the home of the brave. The dust was the enemy.

It could go anywhere, get into anything. The dust was more to be feared than the sudden blinding light or the towering mushroom cloud. With neither a mind nor a soul, the dust was existential evil.

Impelled by the lust for power, the most corrosive element in human nature, the pale brown dust formed windrows on fertile soil which would render it sterile for generations.

The instigators of this atrocity had dozens of excuses for what they had done. But there was only one word for it.

At the end of the hall on the second floor was a pair of French doors hung with white muslin curtains. When Jack opened them he discovered that part of the flat roof of the porch had been transformed. Beside a wrought iron table, painted white, two matching chairs were strategically angled so occupants could enjoy the view. In places where the paint had weathered away streaks of rust showed through. The boundaries of this pleasant little gallery were delineated by flower boxes containing the desiccated remains of long-extinct flowers.

Jack thought he was alone until Edgar spoke up behind him. "This was Veronica's idea; she imagined it was a balcony in Paris. She always dreamed of going to Paris but her health was fragile, so we didn't make it; a brief trip to New York was all she could manage. She insisted on getting a passport anyway. When I asked her why, she said it was important to have big dreams.

"We liked to bring our drinks out here after dinner and watch the sun go down. Veronica said it was better than having a Turner landscape because this was our own private masterpiece."

In his mind's eye Jack could see a gently rolling countryside with a verdant patchwork of fields and forest leading toward the shimmer of a distant lake. That particular view would not have been visible from any other part of the house, but on a summer evening like this . . .

Not today, though.

Seen from this viewing point, today the earth was a gaping wound torn open with a savagery beyond imagining; a reddish-brown scar where every recognizable object had been buffeted and burned. Denuded trees pointed heavenward like accusing fingers. Row after row of the smashed structures of man testified to the futility of trying to erect something permanent when change was the only constant. Blackened pits like the mouths of hell yawned at the invaded sky.

Edgar stood at Jack's shoulder. "Damn them," he said with glacial fury. "Veronica believed in the spirit of place. Did you ever read *Lost Horizon* by James Hilton? Shangri-La was a mysterious monastery in a high mountain valley where no one ever got sick, and people lived for centuries. Soppy movie but a great book. Veronica loved it; she believed every word. When the doctors told us she was terminally ill she talked of going to Tibet, so we could find . . ." His voice trailed away.

Jack was careful not to look at him. He didn't want to see the tears in the older man's eyes.

A gasp informed him that the rest of the group had followed them, crowding onto the porch roof to stare horror-struck at the devastation.

"It's a good thing we didn't see this when we first came out of the barn," Gloria said. "We'd have turned around and gone back underground."

"The shoulder of the hill hid it," Gerry told her.

"Thank God for small mercies. Do you think the rest of the country looks like this?"

"A lot of it may," said Jack. "My guess is, what we're seeing is the new reality."

Nell put one hand over her mouth to stifle a gasp. Jack tried to take her in his arms but she pushed him away.

Pushed him hard.

Nell Bennett was small-boned and elegant, with wide-set eyes that had inspired Jack to comment the first time he saw her, "She looks like a deer caught in the headlights."

His aunt Bea used to say, "Jack's been chasing girls since he found out they were different from boys," but Nell had changed all that. Since falling in love with her, Jack considered wide-set eyes a primary requisite for female beauty.

Strangers assumed Nell was fragile but she was not. She had endured years of marriage to the dictatorial Robert Bennett without letting him subsume her individuality. After his death in the explosion at his factory, she had built a new life on her own terms.

She lowered her hand from her face. "No, Jack, I'm not going to be a baby about this; take it as it comes, you said, and you're right. What made the noise we just heard?"

"A piece of guttering probably broke off the roof."

"All by itself?"

"No, the wind could have blown it loose; there could be dozens of explanations. Small aftershocks are still affecting the ground, it's like what happens after a major volcanic eruption."

"This long after the bombing?"

"I'm not an expert on post-nuclear conditions, Nell."

She gazed past him at the ruined land, mentally picturing it as it might have been before. "Before" had become a word of epic significance, shorthand for an era that had vanished.

A lot of shorthand had been incorporated into the language; veils to camouflage the unmentionable.

A somber group assembled in the living room later. No formal meal was prepared or offered; people wandered into the kitchen and helped themselves to anything that remained edible. Crackers still sealed in a cardboard box, tin cans of soup and beans and fruit cocktail.

The inside of the capacious fridge-freezer smelled appalling; its contents were enshrouded in green fuzz. Bea emptied everything into a garbage bag that she set outside the back door. In the back of a cupboard she found a box of baking soda to use for scrubbing the appliance; she also made a mental note to look for glass jars to preserve fruit and vegetables.

"I could sure go for a couple of fried eggs," Shay said.

"Never had fresh eggs here," Edgar replied. "Veronica was allergic to them."

"Was she allergic to chickens too?"

"No, we both liked to eat chicken, but she couldn't stand the idea of keeping an animal just to kill it." Edgar opened a cupboard and peered inside. "No Jamaican Blue Mountain coffee either," he lamented.

"You drank the last of it during our first week in the shelter," Bea said.

"Why didn't you stop me?"

"Hannibal on an elephant couldn't have stopped you from drinking your coffee."

He looked chagrined. "I thought we'd be able to get more soon."

"Remind me to put that on the list of things we'll need for next time."

"You and your lists," Edgar chided. "Grocery lists, dry cleaning lists, errands to run . . ."

"They keep me organized. Without my lists I'd be lost."

The bedrooms had been appointed to the couples: Jack and Nell, Gerry and Gloria, Shay and Lila, Edgar and Bea. Sleeping arrangements had been organized for the youngsters as well, but no one wanted to go to bed.

The approaching summer evening was unseasonably chill. Instead of normal twilight the sky was an unhealthy green stained with streaks of black cloud. Edgar and Gerry carried in a load of firewood and soon had a blaze dancing on the hearth, but it did not lift their spirits.

Lila stared morosely into a Waterford crystal tumbler holding the last of her host's hoarded Irish whiskey. "We may be the only ones left."

"No way," said Jack. "We'll find a lot of people in Sycamore River."

"I'll bet tons got killed over there," Philip said with relish. "Heaps and piles of spilled guts and burned skin and . . ."

"That's enough, Philip," Gloria told her adopted son. "You're too old to be so ghoulish, and if there are any dead bodies you don't need to see them."

"But I've never seen a dead body!"

"Me neither," his twin rejoined.

"You've never jumped out of an airplane in flight either, but believe me, you wouldn't want to."

The twins were easily distracted. "Are there any airplanes still flying? Didn't all the metal . . ."

"Not all of it," Jack said. "When the Change occurred ten years ago, one of the most puzzling mysteries was that it didn't affect objects uniformly. A lot of compound metal disintegrated but there seems to have been enough left to manufacture some weapons, which is a damned shame when you think about it. If the Change was going to hit us in the gut, I don't know why it didn't go all the way and roll us back to the Stone Age."

"I used to think science had an explanation for everything," Gerry commented.

His wife said, "And I thought God was the answer. It looks like we were both wrong. The God I believed in wouldn't have let this happen."

"Don't give up your faith, Muffin. It's one of the things I love about you."

"You think God is a comforting myth. You want me to sustain it for you just in case it might be true."

He was taken aback by the edge in her voice. While they were underground they had learned to hold their tempers. It seemed petty to give vent to personal anger when the ultimate expression of rage was being expressed overhead.

Gerry argued, "I never said that and I don't think God's a myth, I have the greatest respect for your faith. I just wish I shared it."

Gloria was not easily placated. "You can't be inoculated with faith, and you can't catch it like the common cold either. But if you have as much faith as a grain of mustard seed you can move mountains."

"Who said that?" asked Kirby.

"The Bible."

"Is there anything in the Bible about souls?"

"Why?"

"Millions of people died in the war. What happened to all those souls? Is that what ghosts are: souls?"

Kirby was sitting on a leather hassock by the hearth, with his long legs stretched out in front of him. Gloria could see only one side of his face, the unspoiled side. That young man looks like an angel, she thought. His curly hair and those long dark eyelashes; girls would kill for those eyelashes. "Perhaps you're right, Kirby."

"You believe in ghosts, then?"

"I don't know about ghosts but I do believe in souls. The human soul isn't a religious invention, it's a tiny particle of the energy that animates the universe."

"Do you mean God, Gloria?"

"I mean all creation."

Edgar had been listening to this exchange with steepled fingers under his chin and bright eyes peering from beneath tangled eyebrows. "Souls, spirits, creation . . . are those words interchangeable?" he challenged. Before anyone could answer he said, "When we bring things up from the shelter we'll be sure to include my dictionaries, especially the *Oxford English*. Let's see what the *OED* has to say on the subject, Kirby."

"If we still had computers we could look up the definitions on the internet."

"And where do you think the internet gets its definitions from? They have to be sourced, the computer can't create them. Computers can't create."

Kirby turned to confront Edgar full face. "Oh no? What about AI?"

"Artificial Intelligence uses existing data that requires a computer to extrapolate. Extrapolation's not a creative act. It's like a detective putting together clues."

"Extrapolate!" Gerry snapped his fingers. "That's the word. Refining, smelting and vulcanizing all rely on binding the carbon atom through heat and pressure; knowing that, we can extrapolate that something similar may have been behind the Change."

"You won't give up on that puzzle, will you?" Jack said. "Let me remind you of something. *We're* a carbon-based life-form. As the cosmos developed its clockwork, for want of a better term, so did the carbon atom. Human evolution is pinned to a self-limiting clock."

"Why am I not surprised?"

"It's only an amateur's speculation, but without solid facts it's as good as any other theory. Columbus sailed to the New World on speculation. If he were alive today he would be very surprised."

"Maybe not; even in his time war was a constant. We're so damned determined to exterminate ourselves. . . ."

"It's a safe bet that neither side wanted total annihilation, Gerry. Some miscommunication probably set off a spiraling chain of events that went out of control. This country was targeted by nuclear missiles but there were ordinary bombs too; there was an effort avoid total devastation. The enemy wanted to have enough of America left to be worth the war."

"If that's what they wanted," said Shay, "they shouldn't have used their nuclear capabilities."

"It's not the nukes that did the damage," Edgar retorted.

"What are you talking about?"

"Nuclear weapons can't start a war all by themselves. Politicians can; they're the greatest danger to the world."

Evan could not resist joining in. "We have to have governments, otherwise there'd be anarchy."

Edgar snapped, "Anarchy, my left foot! What do you think Washington is now? I don't mean the city, we all know what happened to it. I mean the national government. Most politicians are all about self-interest: *me, myself and I.* That's the only loyalty they have. When we handed over the country to people like that we guaranteed things would go pear-shaped."

"Speaking of government," Lila interjected, "according to the shortwave there's talk of having another election, though I don't see how one could be organized right now. But anger against the politicians is growing by the day. Voters want candidates who promote peace rather than war."

"And pigs will fly," Edgar said flatly. "As long as the munitions industry makes a huge profit, peace will be off the agenda indefinitely, or at least until all the nukes are destroyed. Was it Einstein who predicted the fourth world war would be fought with stone axes and clubs?"

"An election," Jack mused. "With the mess things are in now, how does anyone think they can organize an election?"

"Restoring the national power grid should be the number one priority," said Lila.

Edgar frowned at her. "Electricity's like a god to you, isn't it? Let me remind you: we were doing okay in the shelter without the national grid."

"We were doing okay with your industrial generator as long as we had fuel for it, but it wouldn't have supplied the rest of our lives. The national grid will enable America to get back to business, which is the lifeblood of this country. Maybe I'll be a newspaper reporter again." Lila paused for a moment, then gave an impish grin. "Come to think of it, there is a down side. When communications are fully restored we'll be positively bombarded with politicians making promises. I'm almost sorry I went to the trouble of bringing home the shortwave when the newspaper office closed down."

"What about the telly?"

"The wallscreen in this house will carry political programs too—unless Edgar can find a way to block them automatically."

"I can sure try. Every gadget on this property's endured my tender ministrations at one time or another, Lila. I cobbled together that smartphone you carry, remember?"

"AllCom. It's an Allcom."

Edgar uttered a humorless laugh. "Not anymore it's not. The devices it used to connect with are long gone. It won't operate your household appliances or bring you the latest weather forecast anymore."

"I can give you a weather forecast," said Bea. "Radiation fallout continues. Look at that dog."

She gestured toward Rocky, who had been lying beside Nell's chair. The Irish setter was struggling to get to his feet. He was panting heavily and drooling long strings of saliva. "Did he pick up something while we were outside? One of those dead birds, maybe?"

"That's it." Jack stood up. "Keep all the dogs and cats indoors from now on. Find some old newspapers to make litter boxes for the cats, and never let a dog go out unless he's on a leash."

Jess threw herself on the floor beside the setter. Her eyes brimmed with tears. "Is Rocky going to be okay?"

Shay bent over the dog and thumbed back an eyelid. "I think so; wild birds aren't very big, even if one died of radiation your dog probably couldn't have eaten enough to kill him. But if you can find some mustard in the kitchen and stir a little into warm water we'll make him vomit, just to be sure."

When Rocky emptied the contents of his stomach onto the floor Shay examined them thoroughly, "It was only a small bit; he'll be okay."

"Do animals have souls?" Kirby wondered.

Jack told him, "No one knows."

"I hope they do. When Sandy and I were kids and Buster was just a baby—before the twins were born—we had a puppy called Skipper. He was white with floppy ears and brown spots and he used to sleep in my bed with me. In the morning he licked my face to wake me up so we could play together. I really loved that dog; maybe more than I realized at the time.

"One day Skipper wandered out in the street and got run over. Mom—our birth mother, I mean—said it's what he deserved for being stupid. She would never let us have another dog, but I'd like to see Skipper again, even as a ghost."

Kirby stared into space, selecting an incident from the vault of childhood memory. "Years later a crazy man who didn't know Tricia shot her dead in town for no reason, and it served her right."

His words startled Gloria. Out of respect for their pain she had never discussed the violent death of their natural mother with the boys, but if Kirby was any indication, perhaps the wounds didn't go as deep as she had thought.

Or perhaps Kirby wasn't as angelic as he appeared.

3

Over their protests, the youngsters were sent to bed. After they left the room, Bea wondered aloud if they would have nightmares.

"I'm going to have nightmares myself," said Gloria. "It's a miracle the horror of it came so close and we're still alive."

"That's what's important," Jack reminded her. "A lot of people anticipated the war and made preparations, though perhaps nothing as elaborate as Edgar's bolt-hole."

"I'm not sure we should let others know we exist . . . I mean let them know our supplies exist," Edgar amended.

Nell said, "Of course we'll share what we have, and be glad there's someone to share with. It would be twice as awful if we were the only ones left alive."

"That's my girl," said Jack. "Always looking for a silver lining."

"I haven't been disappointed yet."

"Far be it from me to spoil your winning streak, but let me point out something to you. In the first half of this century the World Health Organization claimed ninety percent of the people on the planet were breathing polluted air. We were practically choking on our own waste products. There was more plastic rubbish in the oceans than fish, and a whole sub-continent of the stuff floating in the Pacific. Pollution was corroding the stones of the Coliseum and staining the Taj Mahal greenish yellow.

"Then came the Change. Items made out of plastic melted. That didn't last very long, but when it dwindled away, compound metals began to disintegrate. For some reason no one could explain objects stored underground survived; however heavy industry was forced to shut down. There's your silver lining, Nell. When fossil fuels and other toxins were no longer pouring into the atmosphere the air quality was bound to improve. It may have been too late to stop the planet from overheating, but at least we can see more stars at night."

Edgar said sourly, "It's a pity we didn't take time to enjoy them. We were too hell bent on using our damned weapons before they could fail us."

"What do you mean, 'we'?" Evan asked. "No one knows who fired the first shot."

"It doesn't matter," Edgar retorted, "it was going to happen anyway. After the Second World War the politicians and their generals started proxy wars all over the globe. To keep their hand in, so to speak. Warriors have to war, that's what the sons of bitches love. Of course the bigwigs stayed safe while the little guys were doing the fighting and dying. For a helluva long time their leaders resisted using the nuclear option, but the guy who has a superior weapon can't resist showing it off. My hands are bigger than yours, my prick's longer than yours."

"Come on, Edgar," Lila protested. "War isn't a strictly male prerogative."

"I grant you, some women have their share of testosterone, but most of them design skyscrapers and run marathons. It's the male of the species who insists on mortal combat to prove himself. Luckily, in today's world that's only a small percentage compared to the massive armies that used to fight."

"If you think small doesn't matter," Lila shot back, "try being locked in a room with a single mosquito."

Edgar chuckled, a sound akin to the rattle of pebbles. "I know when I'm outmaneuvered. But the fact remains, we can't change human nature. We have to live with it. That's why I built my fallout shelter. Remember the game: 'If you were going to be marooned on a desert island, what would you take?' Well, you're the folks I chose to bring with me. Only a few, you'll notice."

Shay said, "You don't have a very high opinion of the human race, do you?"

"Recent events have proved me right."

"Unfortunately," Nell observed, "we may be left without enough people to repopulate the world."

"It's a mighty big planet. For all the people who've been killed, millions will survive. A llama breeder in Peru may not even realize there was a war."

"It's a mighty small and fragile planet," Gloria contradicted. "Remember the photographs the astronauts took from space? Our beautiful blue marble."

After retiring to the bedroom allotted to herself and Shay, Lila set up the shortwave and began fiddling with dials. At first all she could get was static. Shay looked over her shoulder. "There's no one out there," he said somberly.

"Yes, there is. I just heard . . . no, wait . . . there it is again. A voice . . ." She turned to Shay with her face alight. "Listen!"

He crouched down beside her. "Can you bring it in more clearly?"

"Just give me a minute."

Heads together, the couple listened as eagerly as if they had never heard a human voice. Then Shay went to the doorway and shouted into the hall. "Edgar was right! There are survivors all across the country."

4

The following morning the group returned to the shelter to retrieve their personal belongings. Gloria brought a garden trowel and half a dozen linen dish towels from the kitchen. On the hillside below the barn she collected the dead birds and wrapped them in the towels.

When she saw Kirby watching her, she explained, "I'm going to bury these. Want to help me?"

"Yeah, I guess. I've never touched anything dead before."

"Not even Skipper?"

"*She* tossed him in the garbage can." The way Kirby said "she" conveyed a world of contempt. That young man knows how to hate, Gloria told herself. The accident that left him scarred may have damaged him all the way through.

In the barn Evan harnessed the matched pair of gray Quarter horses, Jupiter and Juno, to the horse-bus, a wooden vehicle Edgar had modeled on an old-fashioned trolley car. When the Change disrupted motorized transportation in Sycamore River, Gerry Delmonico and Shay Mulligan had bought the horse-bus and gone into business together as The River Valley Transportation Service. Evan, who loved horses the way most youngsters his age loved cars and motorcycles, had been one of their drivers. The enterprise was a success from the start. The nostalgic town of Sycamore River loved it.

As inexplicably as it began, the Change had ceased to affect plastic and then compound metals, but the horse-bus had remained popular, even when motorized transport began to be produced again. Cautiously, as if afraid of waking a sleeping giant, manufacturers reopened assembly lines. Entrepreneurs advertised passenger cars employing all the latest innovations and costing a fortune.

Not everyone was willing to pay the price. Some continued to use horses, proudly reminding the doubters, "We don't have to buy gasoline."

Reproducing antique buggies and carriages was only one of Edgar's hobbies. Bea claimed he was constitutionally unable to sit still. A dozen years earlier, when he sold the large engineering firm he had founded, Edgar had insisted on retaining access to machinery and manpower. By then he had become a survivalist. As the clouds of war gathered he had constructed the elaborate arrangement of tunnels he called his "bolt-hole." Based on the ingenious underground constructions of the Germans during the First World War, the tunnels provided safe sleeping quarters, kitchens and sanitary facilities, and could hold enough food and supplies to last a score of people for half a year.

The main entrance to the shelter was camouflaged by the barn which stood above it. "Other folks don't need to know about this," was Edgar's succinct explanation.

Jack and Nell climbed the hill together. Once Nell paused to press her chest with the heel of her hand.

Jack stopped immediately. "What's wrong?"

"A little trouble catching my breath, that's all. It's hot already and this hill's steeper than I thought."

"Not that steep. If it bothers you, tell me what you want from the shelter and go back to the house; I can bring it to you."

"What I really want is my inhaler, but I'm not sure which suitcase it's in."

"I didn't know you used an inhaler."

"I don't as a rule, but I had asthma as a child. They told me I might grow out of it and I did, but once in a great while . . ."

"Look, you go back to the house right now. I'll bring all of your suitcases."

She shook her head. "I won't be pampered, Jack. Let's go on, we're almost there."

Nell had mixed feelings about returning to the shelter. The fear she had endured underground was mitigated by a memory of joy. Facing the possible end of the world had heightened—and accelerated—emotions. Two couples, Jack and herself and Edgar and Bea, had been determined there would be a life afterward. In the heart of the earth they had pledged their wedding vows. No marriage in a cathedral could have been more binding.

Yet when she stood at the top of the steps leading down to the tunnels, Nell felt a moment of trepidation. She had left the shelter only the day before, but already it seemed alien to her, part of a bad dream she could not shake off. She drew a deep breath . . . and became acutely aware of an ache in her chest that spread up to her throat. Simultaneously there was a burning sensation in her nasal passages.

In the shelter they had read about the effects of radiation in Edgar's books and stared in horrified fascination at old photographs from Hiroshima. Anything could be abroad now; any sort of plague or pestilence might have been set loose by the apocalypse.

"Why us?" she whispered to herself, not for the first time. "What did we do to deserve this?"

"Are you going down or staying here?"

"I'm going down, Jack. Only . . ." Her legs buckled abruptly and she sat down hard on the top step. She could taste blood in her mouth.

He bent over her. "You're as white as a ghost! What's wrong?"

"I don't know; delayed reaction, maybe."

Jack straightened up. "Gerry, I'm taking my wife back to the house," he called. "She doesn't feel well; it might be the heat. Tell Gloria, will you? I'd like her to have a look at Nell. And will you find her suitcases and bring them too? Blue hardsiders with name tags on the handles."

Nell was deeply embarrassed. She hated causing a scene, but when Jack made up his mind there was no changing him. He gathered her into his arms and carried her down the hill while Gerry went to find her luggage.

Within the hour Nell was tucked in bed with a glass of water on the nightstand, accompanied by a snifter of brandy. The contents of her suitcases were scattered about the room. Gloria, who had trained as a nurse before she took a degree in psychology, had forbidden Nell to use the inhaler until she determined the cause of the bleeding.

Gerry slouched in the room's only armchair while Gloria gave Nell a cursory examination. She listened to her heart and lungs and took her blood pressure as Jack gazed out a window. A muscle twitched in his jaw.

"It's not asthma," Nell told the room at large. "I know what asthma's like and this isn't it."

"No, I don't think it is," Gloria agreed. "It came on suddenly, you said."

Nell swallowed; winced. "One minute I was fine, then I took a deep breath and felt this pain spread all through my upper body."

"In your lungs?"

"Oh *yes*."

"Is it possible you inhaled a poisonous gas?"

Jack whirled around. "Chemical warfare, you mean? They've already bombed the hell out of us, do you think they're mopping up with . . . No, they'd hardly spray it on empty fields. And we haven't seen any planes or drones or . . ."

Gerry asked, "Has anyone else been affected by it?"

"Not that I know of, but yesterday when we came out of

the barn Lila did remark that the air seemed unusually sharp. That was the word she used: sharp."

"You didn't notice anything more?"

"Maybe I'm not as sensitive as the girls; I have a larger body mass." Jack grinned; a flash of white teeth in tanned face. "How about you, Gloria?"

"I noticed that the air smelled different, but I thought it was because we'd been in the shelter for so long."

Gerry said thoughtfully, "Maybe there has been a change, Jack. Our atmosphere is composed of a number of gases, primarily nitrogen and oxygen, but also argon and small amounts of carbon dioxide, plus traces of methane, ammonia, hydrogen chloride, nitrous oxide, etcetera. You don't want to hear the whole catalog. What's important is this: the proportion of oxygen by volume is twenty-one percent; that's what the human body's adapted to. But the percentage of oxygen in the Earth's crust and the oceans is considerably more than that—and scientists keep revising the figure upward.

"Put it down to climate change or call it anything you like, but the fact remains: the global atmosphere's not a fixed element. It's vulnerable to a lot of factors. We recently exploded god-knows-how-many nuclear weapons. Add the nuclear residue to the detritus of wholesale destruction, give it a stir like the three witches in Macbeth, and what do you have? Possibly something we're not able to breathe. Nell, with your sensitive lungs you could be the canary in the coal mine."

"Stop it," Jack said harshly, "Gerry, you're upsetting her with your speculations."

"They're not speculations, they're perfectly plausible. I worked for Nell's husband as an industrial chemist, remember? I know what I'm talking about. Chemistry, physics, earth sciences, they're all related; everything on Earth is related. The atom is the basic building block. When we began developing nuclear energy we opened a veritable Pandora's Box."

Nell reached for the brandy.

"Hey, don't gulp it like that!"

"I'll drink it anyway I want, Jack."

He took the glass from her hand. "No, you won't. You're going to close your eyes and have a good nap and soon you'll feel better. We'll draw the curtains and leave you alone."

Later, as they were unpacking their things in their own room, Gerry remarked to his wife, "Jack treats Nell like she's made of spun glass, doesn't he? But unless I'm a poor judge of people, she isn't."

"You're a good judge of people, my darling; Nell's a perfectly normal human female."

"Muffin, I haven't been married to a psychologist all these years without picking up a bit of the jargon. Maybe Jack subconsciously wants someone fragile who needs protection. He was raised by his Aunt Bea, a strong, self-sufficient woman if ever there was one. Could be he's looking for her polar opposite."

Gloria gave him a tolerant smile. "Good try, but it's a bit

more complicated than that. The road to the human heart is never straightforward." Her expression turned serious. "I'm going to tell you something and trust you to keep it in strictest confidence."

"You know you can trust me."

"Well . . . all those days and nights we spent in the shelter . . . people talked about everything imaginable. I suspect you men mostly talked about sports and politics, but girl talk is usually personal. When the conversation got around to what we liked in the opposite sex, I remarked that Jack had gorgeous eyes. Bea said, 'I once loved a man with gray eyes, a lecturer at the university. My sister and I both loved him but Florence was more clever than me. She wouldn't give in to him without a wedding ring. I did. By the time I discovered I was pregnant Flo and Campbell were engaged. I wouldn't kill his baby; I left the state the day after their wedding. When my son was born I sent him to the Reeces. They raised him as their own until they were killed in a car crash.'"

Gerry looked at his wife in astonishment. "Do you mean Jack's . . ."

"Bea's son. Yes."

"Does he know?"

"She said she never told him. Some secrets go underground and probably should be left there. They're both mature adults with a long-established relationship. If they were suddenly given a different paradigm, what good would it serve?"

"I'd want to *know*," Gerry insisted.

She glared at him. "And I'll never forgive you if you say a word of this to Jack."

Gerry pantomimed his fingers zipping his lips. Then he unzipped them again. "You really like Jack's eyes? What's wrong with mine?"

Early the following morning, Jack, Gerry and Evan ate a hurried breakfast and prepared for the day ahead. In his shirt pocket Jack had a piece of paper with the addresses in Sycamore River which he wanted to check on. Edgar and Shay would remain in charge at the farm.

Jack said, "We'd better get going before it gets too hot— and before the twins realize we've left. They're wild to see dead bodies."

"Bloodthirsty monkeys," Evan laughed.

"Maybe we should take them with us," said Gerry. "What we're likely to find could be a salutary lesson."

"You're not serious."

"Not really. But when I went to apply for my first driving license we had to walk down a long hallway lined on both sides with police photographs of fatal crashes. No gory detail was spared. It made a profound impression; I've been a careful driver ever since."

When Kirby realized Evan was going to Sycamore River he confronted Jack on the way to the barn. "Why aren't you taking me? There are four horses and I want to see what's happened to our house too."

"I'm sure Gerry will tell you all about it. Besides, one of those horses isn't broken to the saddle."

"I can ride, I love horses."

"That won't impress an untrained colt, Kirby. You'd get dumped before we'd gone any distance."

"You don't know that."

"It's a pretty safe bet," Jack replied. He did not like Kirby's increasingly truculent attitude.

Kirby walked away with his clenched fists thrust deep in his pockets. "Evan thinks he's entitled to everything," he muttered to himself. "Big Shot, always talking about going to Mars. Who does he think he is? Where's he going to get enough money to buy into Mars Settlement?"

Jack and Gerry would ride the horses that pulled the horse-bus. They were versatile animals; two Western saddles covered with carved leather and fitted with saddlebags hung on pegs outside their stalls. Jack chose the gelding called Jupiter, Gerry took Juno. Evan had a lightweight English saddle for Rocket. Shay Mulligan loved show-jumping and so did his son.

When they rode the horses from the barn, Rocket's two-year-old colt whinnied to her. She nickered a soft response but went on.

The journey to Sycamore River began on a short lane at the front of the farmhouse, terminating in an iron cattle guard.

They dismounted to lead their horses across the cattle guard, then mounted again and set off down a graveled road. Startled rabbits bounded away from the roadside.

The men rode past a couple of houses, too suburban in style to be called farms. A folding table in front of one advertised LEMONAID FOR SALE but the proprietor was not tending his business.

When they came to a paved junction, Jack said, "Turn left here, it's the shortest way to Sycamore River. That's about seven miles, as I recall."

Evan told him, "The horses are unshod so they won't slip on the cement, but be careful anyway."

"I know how to ride," Jack replied brusquely.

"I wasn't sure, I've never seen you on a horse."

Jack turned in the saddle to look at him. "I can do a lot of things you've never seen me do." The gray eyes were very cold.

At some point, Evan realized, he had stopped being "Shay's son" to Jack and become a man in his own right. It was an accolade of sorts; almost a rite of passage.

Route 64 cut across a rich stretch of farmland. Byways and country lanes branched off, leading to remote acreage, but more and more houses had been built by the side of the road. Some were pleasant but undistinguished, others were obviously farmhouses. A few had been designed for owners with pretentions. The war had invaded even this rural area. A large field had been cratered by a direct hit. Several farm buildings had been reduced to shards of shattered timber.

The horses began trotting. Evan was a born horseman; he rode head up, shoulders back, torso relaxed and supple, so his body followed every movement of the horse. Jupiter and Juno had the easy jog-trot of Quarter horses, but Rocket was a Morgan-Thoroughbred cross. Her ground-covering stride outdistanced the other two again and again, so Evan had to draw rein and wait for them.

When he paused at a sagging wooden gate in front of a frame house in need of paint, a man emerged from the house: a paunchy, sunburned man wearing dirty denims. There was a week's stubble on his jowls and he was carrying a rifle. He tucked the weapon into the crook of his arm and strode to the gate. "What the fuck do you want here?"

"We don't want anything from you," Jack said. "We're going to Sycamore River to see how they made out over there."

"Why don't you ask how we made out over here? My barn was bombed and all my livestock's dead, that's how. We been fuckin' wiped out. Now how am I supposed to feed my family?" He raked the horses with greedy eyes. "Nice fat mare," he commented, looking at Rocket. "Lot of meat on that one. Pregnant, maybe? An unborn foal'd be mighty tender."

Evan was horrified. "Jack!"

In one fluid movement Jack Reece stepped down from his horse and slipped a pistol from his saddlebag. Aiming the Walther P38 at the head of the farmer, he stated flatly, "That mare belongs to the young man who's riding her. Make a move on her or any of us and it'll be your last."

The farmer froze.

Without putting down the pistol Jack reached for the man's rifle. He skillfully unloaded it with one hand and dropped the cartridges into his pocket. "Take this rifle, Gerry, and drop it on the ground when we've ridden a couple of miles down the road." Shifting his attention back to the farmer, he said in the same deadly tone, "After we're gone you can get your rifle, but don't ever aim it at another human being." Jack remounted Jupiter. "Now get back in your house," he ordered. "Show's over."

"I didn't realize you were carrying a gun," Gerry said as they rode away.

"These days I always have one within reach. That Walther was a souvenir my grandfather brought home from another war. I haven't fired it in a long time, so I wasn't sure it would shoot, but he wasn't sure of his rifle either; did you see how gingerly he was holding it? That's when I knew I had the edge on him."

5

When they came to the river from which the town took its name, they looked at the water with disgust. The Sycamore River had been known for its clarity, providing drinking water for the entire valley. "Clarity" no longer applied. The water was dark, murky, littered with unidentifiable debris.

Rocket stretched her neck down to take a drink but drew back with a snort. Evan patted her sweaty shoulder. "That's okay, babe, we'll find good water in town."

Gerry said, "I wouldn't count on it."

"Isn't there a bridge somewhere along here?"

"Don't count on that either. See that twist of wreckage in the water? I suspect it's what's left of the bridge."

They rode along the riverbank until they came to a shallow ford. The horses picked their way carefully over the riverbed. Rocket shied several times at objects that did not belong in a river. As they reached the opposite bank they caught a whiff of sickly sweet odor that turned Evan's stomach. "Is that . . ." He could not finish the question.

"Our hometown," Jack replied bleakly. "The wind must be blowing this way." If Evan had been alone he would have turned around and gone back, but he could not let Jack Reece think him a coward. He sat quietly in the saddle and gripped Rocket's sides with his legs to steady her. She could smell what he could. She did not like it either.

"Go on," Gerry urged.

Evan tightened his legs. Pressed down with his seat bones. The three horses walked forward, their bodies tense with protest.

Between the river and the town was a strip of parkland equipped with picnic benches, barbecue pits and playground equipment; a popular attraction for local residents. "Riverside" houses commanded high prices on the real estate market.

The most recent visitor to the park had been a ballistic missile.

A large section of earth was badly mauled; the few remaining clumps of grass were scorched and dying. Slides and jungle gyms had been flung about by a giant's hand. One swing set remained upright; the wind was pushing the swings eerily to and fro as if propelled by invisible children. The chains creaked like a creature in pain.

Evan shuddered.

Rocket would not pass the haunted swings. Taking their cue from her, the usually phlegmatic Quarter horses also refused. They flattened their ears against their heads and planted their feet stubbornly in the earth. After a brief and embarrassing tussle the riders dismounted to lead their animals. None of them would risk being bucked off.

They did not remount until they reached the first sidewalk.

Jack took the list of addresses from his pocket. "Looks like your neighborhood's the nearest, Gerry, so we'll start there."

"I'm not sure I want to."

"It's like ripping adhesive tape off a wound. Don't think about it first, just grab it and give it a yank."

The area had suffered badly. Windows were shattered, chimneys collapsed. Doors stood ajar but not in welcome. Streets were cluttered with fallen poles and dangerous wires. In one gutter a dead dog had attracted a swarm of flies. A blizzard of paper blew past in the wind: computer printouts, tax returns, discarded newspapers and forgotten love letters; the records of lives perhaps ended now.

The Delmonico house, a single-storey California rancher, had been extended to accommodate their adopted family. The older part remained but the wing was a pile of rubble. The wooden deck at the back was partially burned; the brick barbecue beside it was unscathed.

"I built that barbecue myself, it took me a whole damned week," Gerry lamented. "Gloria got the instructions off the internet."

"You used to give great deck parties."

"We will again, Jack. Our home insurance policy covers acts of war."

"Have you read it recently?"

Gerry had a sinking feeling. "No, it's with the mortgage. That and our wills are in a safe at our lawyer's office."

"How safe are safes now?" Jack wondered.

The Mulligan home and the veterinary clinic beside it were undamaged. While Jack and Gerry waited, Evan went through them both and came out satisfied. "The damage around here is so random, so hit-and-miss. It doesn't seem fair."

Gerry said, "War isn't fair. We never did anything to those people."

"They may be saying the same thing about us."

"How could they? They were the aggressors."

The office building which housed the law firm that represented the Delmonicos had been destroyed. Gerry poked through the ruins looking for a safe but did not find one. "How am I going to tell Gloria? We thought we were being so sensible."

The streets were increasingly littered with items people had discarded in their headlong flight from the bombs raining on their town. A china doll with a broken head, a scuffed leather briefcase, a framed studio photograph of a smiling family. An oil painting of a seascape that might have been hanging above a living room fireplace.

Jack consulted his list again. "Aunt Bea's place is next."

"Even if something's happened to it," Gerry said, "she won't be homeless, she has the farm."

"I'm not sure she'll see it that way; the house means a lot to her. She inherited it from her parents and I grew up there. There's still an oak tree in the backyard with an old rubber tire hanging from it; I used to swing on that tire and pretend I was in a spaceship going to the moon."

"An interest in space travel is something we have in common, then," Evan told Jack. "We read about the mission to Mercury when I was in school; it really caught my imagination. Japanese and European scientists had collaborated on a vehicle they called BepiColombo, which carried twin probes to study the planet. Of course nobody landed and walked around on the surface, Mercury is a hellish place. But we've actually landed on Mars. We can *live* on Mars; that's what I'd like to do."

Jack said, "I never went to the moon and I don't know if you'll get to Mars, Evan. Wars are expensive; the one we just had may have soaked up all the money for the space program and a lot else as well. It's a good thing the space agency made the exploratory post on Mars self-sufficient, it could be a long time between supply ships."

Gerry said, "They should have hired Edgar Tilbury to do their planning."

In the long-established residential neighborhood where Jack grew up one could almost believe there had never been a war. Most of the houses had changed little over the years. The majority were neat frame bungalows centered on their lawns, or traditional red brick colonials with attached garages. Mature trees lined the street.

Behind a picket fence reinforced with wire a German shepherd broke into furious barking at the horses passing by.

The house Jack knew so well looked the same as always.

Invasive speedwell had taken over the front flower bed.

"She might rent the house out, I suppose," Jack speculated.

"It's a waste to leave it standing empty. So many people who lost their homes are going to be desperate for a place to live."

Gerry said, "Bea sure doesn't need anyone's rent money. Isn't that always the way? When you have money more pours into your lap; when you need it the tap's turned off."

Sycamore River had been a pretty town; it was pretty no longer. It was hardly even a town; the center was mostly ruins. Among them the four stories of Goettinger's Department Store remained proudly upright. The brick façade was blackened except where what appeared to be a pale human shadow was imprinted on one wall.

The Sycamore and Staunton Mercantile Bank was intact as well, though the white marble columns across the front were stained an ashen gray.

"Aunt Bea will be tickled when I tell her they couldn't destroy her bank," Jack said. "She spent her entire working life there; it was like her child. When the Old Man died she was promoted to president."

"I always thought there was something between her and Old Man Staunton," Gerry confided.

"My aunt? You must be joking."

The attack on Sycamore River had been one of the last before the truce was agreed; pilots on their way home had taken advantage of the opportunity to dump materiel that was no longer needed and save fuel. They had left behind a lot of collateral damage.

Most of the dead bodies had been found by search parties and removed, but the smell lingered. The unmistakable stench of decomposition had soaked into the earth, permeating everything. The summer sun was making it worse.

The horses were snorting and skittish. They did not refuse to go any farther, but their tension unnerved their riders.

Gerry said, "I feel like I'm sitting on dynamite that could go off at any time."

The words were barely out of his mouth when Jupiter was startled by a bird suddenly flying out of an open doorway. The horse lunged to one side, slamming into the gray mare. Gerry grabbed Juno's mane to hold on. Her scrambling hind legs dislodged a pile of rubble and a miniature landslide cascaded into the road, uncovering the upper half of a man's body.

The face was burned raw; the eye sockets were hollow. Fluid from the melted eyes had run down the dead cheeks.

Evan slid from his horse and was violently sick.

The ruined cityscape contained too many memories. They had made only a cursory examination when Jack said, "Before we leave I want to ride out to Nell's house, in case she asks about it."

He didn't say "our house" though he had shared it with Nell for months. To Jack it would always be Robert Bennett's house, as grandiose and dominating as the man had been. Jack had planned to build a very different home for Nell.

Before the war.

The mock-Normandy chateau that represented Robert Bennett's opinion of himself dominated a gated enclave west of downtown. It was the largest and without doubt the costliest of the expensive homes built by the town's elite. Although modeled on the style of medieval France, the house was totally automated. A touch of the AllCom had operated everything, from unlocking the baronial front doors to defrosting the large walk-in freezer.

The bomb which struck the Bennett mansion squarely in the middle had not been deterred by its grandeur. Only a portion of the front wall remained standing. It still held the carved double doors with the copper carriage lamps Nell had selected.

Jack gave a wry smile. "Guess I won't have to unlock the doors."

"Hey, I'm sorry about this, Jack."

"Why, Gerry? You didn't do it. And I'm not sorry to see the place turned to rubble." Jack dismounted, gave Jupiter's reins to Evan to hold, and sidled past the front doors.

Most of the wreckage inside the house was recognizable as furniture or structural damage, but one item caught Jack's eye and he bent to retrieve it.

The object was filthy and reeked of smoke.

"What in hell is that?" Gerry asked when Jack carried it outside. All three horses were spooked by it.

"This is, or was, a fur coat," Jack said, holding it at arm's length "Lynx, if I'm not mistaken."

"Aren't lynxes extinct?"

"I don't think so, Evan . . . but if they are, Robert Bennett probably shot the last one. He was a gung-ho trophy hunter."

"As demonstrated by his wife," said Gerry.

"Don't ever let Nell hear that, she hated being called a trophy wife."

"What else could you call it when the richest man in town marries the most beautiful woman in town just to show her off?"

"For all I know, maybe Bennett loved her. It's hard not to. Your own wife's a stunner, Gerry. Do you think of her as a trophy?"

"Gloria'd kill me. Besides, she's not a trophy, she's a witch. You going to bring that thing with us?"

"And give it back to Nell? No way." Jack tossed the fur aside while he remounted. "She never wore it, she said it looked better on the lynx. When we went to the shelter she left a lot of personal belongings here, including all the things he'd given her. Kind of like a snake shedding its skin."

As they rode away from the house Gerry commented, "There wasn't anyone in town who liked Robert Bennett; even me, and I worked for the man. You have to give him some credit, though. He saved Kirby's life when RobBenn blew up and burned to the ground."

Evan asked, "Why did the factory blow up? Hasn't there always been some mystery about it?"

"No real mystery," Jack told him. "The police report was quite explicit, but it's one of those incidents that gets brushed under the rug because so many people could be hurt by it. The RobBenn complex exploded after Kirby and his brothers broke in and started fooling around with the chemicals in Gerry's laboratory. The Delmonico kids had a proclivity for trouble."

"They weren't our kids then," Gerry protested. "They were the Nyeberger boys, a wild bunch who needed love and discipline in equal measure according to my wife. Since we adopted them they've settled down a lot." Gerry glanced at Evan. "What are you sniggering about?"

"You really think those kids have settled down? Sandy went off to the navy so he's their problem now. Kirby and Buster are grown enough to be civilized, but you have no idea what Flub and Dub get up to behind your back. And what did you mean when you called your wife a witch?"

6

"Gloria's enchanting," said Gerry, "but that's not what I meant. My wife . . . how can I put this . . . Gloria's in touch with . . ." Gerry paused again. "You were on the hill, Evan, when she went around and gathered up those dead birds and buried them. It was like a little ritual, wasn't it? To her they were sacred; everything that contains life is sacred. Back when we were high school sweethearts her mother told me she was fey."

"Faye? I thought her name was Gloria."

"F-E-Y. It means unworldly, a visionary. Look it up in one of Edgar's dictionaries, it describes my wife pretty well."

When they returned to the Tilbury farm a crowd was waiting for them. Before they could get off their horses the three men were inundated with questions. "What did you see?" "Was there much damage?" "Is anyone alive over there?"

Jess Bennett stood at Evan's knee, smiling up at him. "I'm so glad you're back, I was worried about you."

For a brief moment those words seemed to be the most important thing that had happened all day. Then he remembered. "I'm all right but it was pretty bad. There was a lot of damage and a lot of people were killed."

Philip Delmonico came running up in time to hear the last. "Lots of corpses?" he asked avidly.

"Sorry, Flub, I didn't see any," Evan lied.

The teenager gave him a shrewd look. "If you did you wouldn't tell me, would you?"

"It's not something I want to talk about."

The older men were kept busy answering questions. "There was no warning," Gerry reported. "Not even an air raid siren. Several hundred people were killed outright, maybe more, not to mention the injuries. Many are still in shock. Some are still just aimlessly wandering around."

Jack added, "Nell's favorite supermarket was flattened. The roof pancaked and crushed everything underneath. We saw a man out in front, sweeping up broken glass with a dustpan and a woman's hairbrush. When I asked him why he bothered he said, 'Our customers will need a place to park tomorrow.' The poor bastard had no idea what tomorrow would be like."

Gerry told Gloria, "No one's staying in the town itself, that wouldn't be safe, but they're putting up tents and erecting shelters in Daggett's Woods. Fortunately most of the hospital's still standing, but it's badly damaged and the emergency wing has been . . ."

Her face lit up. "The hospital wasn't destroyed?"

"That's what I said. It was struck by several conventional bombs, though. They won't be accepting any patients for quite a while."

"I have to go over there; I'll be needed."

"You're needed here, Muffin. Our family depends on you, and it's not just the kids. *I* depend on you."

"We've got friends here to look after you, but in the town . . ."

"What about in the town?" Edgar interrupted. "Gerry, did you tell anyone where you were coming from?"

"No."

"Didn't they ask?"

"Several did, but we managed to change the subject," said Jack. "I understand why you don't want a crowd beating a path to our door. We'd be overwhelmed."

"Who did you meet that you knew?"

"There was Fred Mortenson and Arthur Hannisch . . ."

"A dry cleaner and a jeweler, just what we need," Edgar said drily.

"If the hospital isn't open the survivors in Sycamore River will need trained medical help, so I'm going," Gloria declared. "We have a good stock of medical supplies here; we were lucky we never needed them for ourselves. I'll take them with me."

She was adamant. When Gloria Delmonico made up her mind she was deaf to argument. Eventually it was agreed that she would take the pony and trap—a light cart Edgar had built and which Rocket could pull. The cart would hold two people with a load of medical supplies.

"Rocket has to have a rest first," Evan insisted. "Today she's trotted more than fifteen miles in scorching hot weather."

Gloria reluctantly agreed. "We'll go first thing in the morning, then."

Jack had been watching the young man's face; Evan plainly dreaded going back to Sycamore River. Jack decided, "Gerry, you should drive, Gloria's your wife. And don't follow Route 64; you don't need to tangle with that man who wants to eat horseflesh."

Evan's relief was obvious.

Jess accompanied him as he led Rocket to the barn. "She's a beautiful horse. What color do you call that?"

"Chestnut. Rocket's a chestnut."

"Chestnuts aren't that color."

"I know, but the term's applied to any reddish-brown horse. Rocket's colt is a chestnut too; you've seen him in the barn. Comet's two years old now; strong enough to be trained for riding, but with all that's been going on I haven't had the time."

Jess gave Evan a radiant smile. "Let me help you, I love horses. I've always wanted to learn to ride."

She stayed with Evan while he unsaddled Rocket and rubbed her down. She asked questions about the curry comb and brushes, she bent over to watch Evan wield the hoof pick on the mare's feet. "There's a lot to taking care of a horse," Jess remarked.

"You don't know the half of it. But when you really love . . ." Evan glanced at the girl. His ears went pink.

That night over supper Edgar confessed his disquiet. "I feel sorry for the people in Sycamore River, but their story's being repeated all over the country. What happened will affect us in more ways than we know. At first we thought the Change was just about plastic melting, but the Change is what we're living through, and will for a long time to come.

"Did any of you see one of those hokey Hollywood movies where the American president won a war single-handed and flew a jet fighter home to a flourish of trumpets and a background of stars and stripes? Pure hogwash. We're no longer a nation; when the dust of this war settles we could be a patchwork of villages, or perhaps rogue states, each one out for itself. Somewhere along the way we lost the shining city on the hill. Selfishness became our way of life.

"As Thomas Jefferson once wrote, 'Those entrusted with power have, in time . . . perverted it to tyranny.' Power can be a bludgeon or a surgeon's scalpel. In their pursuit of personal power our so-called leaders told us the lies we wanted to hear. They coarsened the moral fiber of America and made enemies of our allies. Worst of all was the egregious damage they did to the environment in order to line their own pockets. Floods, droughts, massive wildfires . . . all are down to human selfishness.

"I'm an old man and I'm tired. Tired clear through, with holes in my memory and rust in my joints. Actually I'm thankful I won't live to see how America reconstructs herself. Death is the get-out-of-jail card, isn't it? Climate change is making parts of the world uninhabitable already; soon that will include areas of America too. Dealing with the problem will require inspired leadership, a modern Abe Lincoln, and I'm afraid there's no such person available. Instead we only have more of the willful ignorance that got us into this. Americans sure followed the wrong role model."

Jack studied Edgar's deeply lined face. The sharp features sagged, the bright eyes were dull. Bea had confided that he did not sleep well at night. "He takes short naps all day instead. That's what many people do at his age."

7

"Death is the get-out-of-jail card."

Jack recalled those words the following morning when a distraught Bea cried out, "I can't wake up Edgar!" The entire group hurried to their room. There was not enough space inside for all of them, but what was important could be seen from the doorway.

Edgar Tilbury was lying in a fetal position facing toward the door, with his head on Bea's pillow. His eyes were closed; his lips were curved in a faint smile.

Samson lay on the floor close beside the bed, whimpering.

Gloria bent over the bed to take Edgar's pulse. She took a deep breath, waited, checked it again, then turned to Bea. "I'm afraid he's gone. I'm so sorry."

Jack took Bea's elbow and guided her to the nearest chair. Her voice was barely audible. "He said he was tired, that's all. So very tired. And he was, he could hardly put his pajamas on." Dry-eyed, Bea looked up at Jack. "He always wore both the tops and bottoms, did you know that? He didn't want me to see his wrinkled old body. As if it would make any difference! I have a wrinkled old body too but he insisted I was beautiful. Beautiful."

The tears began to flow then. Jack had never seen Bea weep before.

Gloria gently pulled the sheet over Edgar's face.

"We were going to grow old together," Bea murmured. "Like the poem: 'Grow old along with me! The best is yet to be . . .'"

Jack huskily recited, "The last of life, for which the first was made."

She swallowed hard. "I was looking forward to getting old with Edgar. He was my reason to get up in the morning. He had a quirky sense of humor; he didn't like jokes but he enjoyed riddles. He could be tender too, though I doubt if any of you saw that side of him. We remembered the same songs; the same *world*. If he's gone that's gone.

"When we went to bed he always put his head on my shoulder. He did last night. The last thing he said to me, was 'Good night, Veronica.'"

Bea's voice broke. She buried her face in her hands.

Lila Ragland was inconsolable. She collapsed in Shay's arms and could not stop sobbing. "Edgar was the best friend I ever had. I'm a genius on the computer but when he took me in I was running wild. Without him I might be in prison now, or worse. He encouraged me to change, which is why I went to work for the newspaper. I became a different person thanks to Edgar. What am I going to do without him!"

Shay had heard it all before. He recognized the babble of grief.

They left Bea alone for a while, sitting with Edgar. By the time she rejoined them she was herself again—though her eyes were still red. Samson followed her like a shadow.

In the living room the group discussed the arrangements that must be made. Gloria's trip to Sycamore River was tacitly postponed. Jack said, "Aunt Bea, you can take your time about this, but have you given any thought to Edgar's . . ."

"Final resting place? Not yet. My family owns several grave sites at Sunnyslope."

"That's where I first met Edgar," Lila volunteered. "He was visiting . . ."

"His first wife's grave, I know. It could be the perfect place." No matter how much pain it cost Bea, what Edgar might have wished had to be paramount; this was the last service she could render him.

"She isn't there now," Shay said.

"What are you talking about?"

Shay would not meet Bea's eyes. "Veronica isn't buried in Sunnyslope; Edgar told me himself. She was at first, but he didn't want to have her so far away from the place she loved. He paid someone to help him move her. Her grave is in the hill above the bomb shelter."

"Are you certain?"

"Absolutely."

Bea bristled. "That can't be true; Edgar would have told me."

"Even in the best marriages," Gerry observed, "there are

secrets. He might have been trying to spare your feelings. You said he was tender."

Kirby had been following this conversation with keen interest. "When we were down in the shelter there was a dead woman above us?" the young man asked. "Like a guardian angel?"

Jack decided the first thing to do was to locate the grave on the hill to be certain it was there. "Burying a body on private property without legal documentation is against the law in most states, and Edgar was a prudent man. There'll be no headstone on the site."

"So how do you find someone who's been secretly buried for years?" Gerry wanted to know. "It's not like witching for water."

"We'll simply have to go up there and hunt for it. If she meant so much to him he must have placed a symbol somewhere. Anyone want to come with us to help?"

Gloria said, "If my husband's going I'm going too."

Samson continued staying close to Bea. He looked at her with such tragic eyes she was certain he knew what had happened. She insisted she was a cat person, but there was no way she would rebuff Edgar's dog. And no way she would join the others in the search for Veronica's grave. She waited in the house with Samson.

From time to time she looked out the kitchen window and toward the barn.

You'll always be there, Mary Veronica Tilbury, she said silently to the presence on the hill. Edgar showed me his will; he left everything to me, including the ground you lie in. He must have assumed I'd want to live in this house. Your house. It's funny the things men don't think of; they're always surprised when women get upset. Edgar wasn't cruel, he might have intended to make other arrangements but I'll never know. He was tough, he expected to have more time. We all expect to have more time until we come bang up against the wall.

Bea went to the bedroom and the sheeted figure on the bed. Samson followed her. After turning around three times he settled himself on the rug beside the bed and began chewing the fringe. He rolled his eyes toward Bea to see if she was going to scold him but she was paying no attention.

She continued her silent monologue. Does it make any difference where a body is buried, Edgar? The spirit is what matters. If I weren't such a coward I'd come with you. I can't because it would hurt Jack too much. We'll be facing some very tough times and I want to be here for him.

When the search party returned Jack was exultant. "We found it, Aunt Bea! We would have missed it except for Gloria, she called our attention to it. There are wildflowers on the hill, and nearest the top is a patch of that weed you call speedwell. When I was a boy you had me dig it out of your garden because it was so invasive."

Gloria said, "That weed is a popular choice for planting in rock gardens and dry ground because it's almost indestructible. The blossoms are small but very beautiful. Garden centers label it as 'Veronica.'"

8

The coffin would be homemade, using materials from Edgar's workshop. As a soft background accompaniment for the funeral Bea selected Pachelbel's "Canon in D Major" from Edgar's vast collection of records and CDs. He would be dressed in his best suit, the one he wore when they were married. In the absence of a clergyman Jack offered to conduct the service. "I've been to enough funerals, I know the drill."

Bea gave him the family Bible and prayer book from which to read. Jack's name was on the page that contained his family tree; his parents were listed as Cameron and Florence Reece.

The new widow need not seek official permission to bury Edgar beside Veronica. Unsanctioned graves were being dug all over the country. In the scorching hot weather people were anxious to get their mangled and mutilated loved ones tucked into the earth.

When the time came, Bea steeled herself as best she could. She dressed in a gray silk dress that complemented her silver hair, and around her neck she wore a single strand of pearls. Real pearls, not cultured.

She wanted everything to be the way Edgar would like it.

When the day predictably dawned hot and sunny, Bea was disappointed. She preferred for funerals to take place on cool rainy days to match the mood of the occasion, but such days had become a rarity. The coffin was carried up the hill on the shoulders of Edgar's friends. Bea walked behind them with her hand tucked in the crook of Kirby's arm. "Looking after the widow is more important than being a pallbearer," he boasted to Jess Bennett.

Samson followed the entourage with his head down and his tail between his legs.

Near the top of the hill was the neatly dug grave. Two flat gravestones were already in place. Bea had ordered them to be devoid of dates; she did not know the dates for Edgar's first wife. Her stone bore only the words "Mary Veronica Tilbury." Edgar's, also dateless, identified the person to be buried there as "Edgar George Tilbury." After giving the matter considerable thought she had decided against adding anything else.

The stones were surrounded by intensely blue flowers.

Afterward Bea recalled almost nothing about the actual funeral except for Jack's voice reciting, ". . . the kingdom and the power and the glory, Amen." It was as if a veil had been hung between her and the pain. As she started down the hill toward the house the world came back into focus. "Go on now," she said to Kirby, "I'll be all right. I just want to be alone for a bit."

He looked doubtful but did as she asked.

Bea was not allowed the reflective time she sought, because

almost immediately Gloria joined her. "I hope I did the right thing by identifying those flowers. I'm an obsessive gardener, and . . ."

"No, no, it was lucky you recognized them," Bea replied. "Do you suppose Edgar planted them on purpose? Or did they grow there on their own?"

"We'll never know. Probably just a coincidence."

Bea said, "A long time ago I read, 'Coincidence is God's way of remaining anonymous.'"

Gloria smiled. "I like that."

"Are you religious?"

"Gerry and I used to go to church regularly and the children were baptized there, but I think it was more about tradition than conviction. In Sycamore River our friends and family went to church so we did too. But the war . . ."

"Yes. The war. It's become the reason for so many things, not least of which is the loss of faith in God."

"I haven't rejected my faith, Bea, only institutionalized religion. Personally I believe the Creator is present in all his works, in the spirit of every living thing and in the cosmos itself. I find evidence wherever I look."

"Then I'm not looking in the right places; maybe I'm too much of a skeptic," said Bea. "But there has to be something, doesn't there? The entire universe can't be a gigantic accident, it defies logic. What about the Big Bang, where did that come from?"

"Kirby has a theory about that." Gloria glanced around to

make sure he was out of earshot. "He's such a funny young man, you'd never know what goes on in that odd head of his. When he was thirteen or fourteen he announced the Big Bang was because God blew up."

In spite of herself, Bea laughed. "Thank you for brightening a sad day. Come into the kitchen with me, Gloria, and lend a hand. I'm going to make sandwiches and iced tea for everyone."

The mourners gathered in the living room, thankful to be out of the hot sun. The refreshments were greeted with a hearty welcome. "We played Edgar's favorite music," said Lila, "so we should drink a toast to him in his favorite Irish whiskey. He's the one who taught me the Irish spell whiskey with an 'e.' But I'm afraid I drank the last of it."

"Iced tea is a better idea on a day like this," Shay assured her. He lifted the top slice of his sandwich and peered at the contents. "What do you call this? Some kind of hash?"

Bea tilted her head back to stare at him through the spectacles on her nose; the same chilly gaze she had used on loan applicants in the bank. "I call it Luncheon Luxury. It consists of selected leftovers from the food I prepared earlier in the week. If you don't want it now I'll assume you didn't want it then either. If that's the case, perhaps you'd like to take over the cooking?"

Shay took a big bite and forced a smile even before he swallowed.

The room was relatively quiet while they ate; the room Veronica had decorated. While they were at the grave site Bea had been almost painfully aware of the woman who slept beneath the blue flowers.

"Two ghosts now," Bea said under her breath.

"What?"

"Nothing."

Kirby left the room and returned with a copy of the *Oxford English Dictionary* under his arm. He set it down on the glass coffee table and began thumbing through it like someone accustomed to dictionaries. When he found what he was looking for he read aloud, "'Soul is the spiritual or immaterial part of a person, regarded as immortal.'"

"Then what's the definition for spirit?" Jack asked.

Kirby found the answer moments later. "'Spirit is the nonphysical part of a person which is the seat of emotion and character, and is regarded as surviving after the death of the body.'"

"Does it have to be a person? Can a place have a spirit? Edgar once referred to 'the spirit of place.'"

"Places have character all right," said Gerry, "and they can project a sort of emotion. That park outside Sycamore River, with the empty swings . . ."

Evan shuddered. "Let's not talk about that."

Lila said, "It's interesting, the sort of conversations people have after a funeral. We think about things we try to ignore otherwise, but if the talk's going to get serious I want another glass of tea with a slug of sloe gin in it. Anyone else?"

When their glasses had been refilled the conversation resumed where it left off. Bea said, "What exactly constitutes a spirit of place?"

"It's hard to define," said Gerry, "but you could put me down on any street in Manhattan and I'd know where I was right away."

"Or London, or Paris," Jack elaborated.

"That's because they all have landmarks; you can't ignore the Empire State Building or the Eiffel Tower. But what about places without any human constructions? Is there a spirit of place for the Rocky Mountains?"

"Indubitably. And one for the moon."

"And another for Mars Settlement," Evan interjected.

Jess Bennett gave him a quizzical look. "I didn't know you were interested in space travel."

"Well, I am, always have been."

"I thought you were going to stay here and teach me to ride horses."

While Evan struggled to think of a response, Gloria turned to Nell. "How're you feeling?"

"Better, but my chest and throat still bother me. Your husband suggested our atmosphere was changing, and I might be the proverbial canary in a coal mine."

"Gerry, what a mean thing to say!"

"I wasn't being mean, Muffin, but I'm a scientist. The rate of carbon dioxide molecules per cubic meter in the atmosphere has diminished drastically since the collapse of heavy industry, and the percentage of oxygen is increasing. We could be approaching a dangerous atmospheric imbalance. The problem is, we've become gradually acclimated to increasing atmospheric pollution since the dawn of the industrial revolution. If it's going the other way now . . . well, we'll just have to adjust."

"Won't less carbon dioxide have a negative effect on plant life?"

"Undoubtedly. Most plants take in carbon dioxide and give off oxygen; that's why I worry about a dangerous imbalance. So many things humans do can upset the balance of nature."

"So the air we breathe could be even worse for us than politicians."

"Now you're teasing me, but there is truth in what you just said. We could do without politicians but we can't do without air."

9

Late in the afternoon, when the worst of the heat had abated, Evan saddled Rocket and went for a ride. He headed in the opposite direction from Route 64.

When he had a lot on his mind he found being alone with his horse therapeutic. The death of Edgar Tilbury had rocked him. It was the first death in Evan's circle of friends and relatives, and had left a surprising hole. Edgar had been like a grandfather; an exceptionally wise grandfather and a font of wisdom.

Evan was aware he had come to a fork in the road; the first major decision he had ever faced.

For as far back as he could remember he had dreamed about space. When he outgrew childhood it was one of the few dreams he brought with him. Mars Settlement, which had only been in the planning stage when he was a boy, excited him more than anything else, even horses.

When the first exploratory flights to Mars began he had taken his telescope into the backyard on clear nights and peered for hours at the Red Planet. He didn't expect to see the fabled canals—space probes in the last century had disproved that myth—but he could envision other aspects. Shifting dunes of crimson sand; towering volcanoes. Spaceports with flame-tailed ships like silver bullets.

A world nothing like Earth.

Shay had always hoped his son would join him in his veterinary practice, but the long period of study, equal to that for a medical doctor, had been too daunting. Evan was too ready for life to spend any more of it in schools. While he waited for his future to unfold he sometimes helped his father in the clinic, but had never taken the work seriously.

Then the war broke out.

The men and women comprising the Russo-American geological force to survey the planet and determine the best sites for settlement were stranded on Mars. Evan envied them. They had a brand new world to explore while he was stranded in dull old Sycamore River. Disappointment gnawed at him.

Now the war was over. Or at least there was an armistice, though Edgar had not shown a lot of faith in it. Evan felt certain the work on Mars Settlement would resume soon.

The first radio announcement excited him so much he could not sleep. The voice on the evening news had been like a clarion call from heaven. "Emigration rolls for Mars Settlement will be opening in twelve months' time. The first will be limited to strategic personnel, but all who wish to apply as colonists are advised to contact the space agency for further details. It is envisioned that actual settlement may begin within five years."

Jess Bennett wanted him to stay on Earth with her.

When a courier delivered a large envelope bearing the insignia of the space agency Evan took it straight to his room and closed the door. He was so eager to rip open the envelope that he tore a corner off the detailed list of requirements for prospective settlers. He made himself slow down and read carefully.

He could not take his horse to Mars, although farms to help make the colony self-sustaining were being planned for the future. Arrangements would be made for importing livestock in embryo; primarily breeds of cattle, sheep and pigs able to adapt to Martian conditions. Colonists with a background in agriculture would be given special consideration for emigration.

Married couples also would be encouraged, provided they were young and fit and both had skills that would be needed on Mars.

Evan could argue that his knowledge of caring for large animals was valuable, and determined to start studying his father's old textbooks immediately. Jess was interested in English literature but pioneers on Mars would not require a knowledge of Shakespeare and Chaucer. She might not be considered as acceptable at all.

Fork in the road.

Evan let Rocket meander at her own pace with the reins lying loose on her neck and his mind literally millions of miles away. When twilight fell he still had not come to a decision. Evan picked up the reins and clucked to his horse. "We better go home, Rocket. Supper's waiting."

At the table Lila announced, "Homeland Security's broadcasting again, there have been food riots in several cities. They're urging people to avoid the major population centers until troops are in place to restore order. *The Boston Globe* will be publishing casualty lists soon. Meanwhile the Red Cross is organizing food banks and . . ."

Shay asked, "Why *The Globe*? Why not *The New York Times*?"

"It seems *The Times* publishing plant was destroyed but *The Globe*'s still in business. Boston didn't take as hard a hit as New York and . . ."

"How are we supposed to get the newspapers?" Bea interrupted. "There's no home delivery and, so far, the postal service only carries business mail."

"For now the papers are being shipped in bulk to the major population centers."

Gerry gave a derisive snort. "The same ones we're told to avoid? Snafu."

"What's that?" Kirby asked.

Jack said, "It's an acronym dating back to the Second World War. Snafu is short for 'Situation Normal, All Fucked Up' which is a pretty accurate description of our government today."

That night in bed Evan added the condition of the government to the other elements in his equation. What had Edgar said? "Inspired leadership, a modern Abe Lincoln."

Edgar had been scathing in his condemnation of politics but Lincoln was a statesman. So were Jefferson, Reagan, McCain.

They came from differing backgrounds but they had three things in common: personal integrity, a deep love of their country and an unshakeable loyalty to the Constitution.

I could meet those qualifications. I studied civics and political science in school and got good grades.

I got good grades in science too.

I could marry Jess, I could become a vet, I could go to Mars. Some but not all of those things.

Evan lay on his back with his arms folded under his head and gazed with unseeing eyes at the ceiling. Far beyond that ceiling the stars waited.

What should I do? What would Edgar advise if he were still here?

In the velvet deeps of night, at last Evan Mulligan rolled over and slept.

Before breakfast in the morning he fed and groomed the horses, then returned to the house for his own breakfast. Afterward he took the last piece of cooling toast to his room and munched on it while he hunted out a box of white paper. The mahogany table in the dining room already had been cleared. Bea would polish it before the next meal; she took scrupulous care of everything in the house. Through the open doorway to the kitchen Evan could hear the sounds of dishes being washed and put away in the cabinets.

Sitting down at the table, he took out a sheet of paper and stared at its blank face until words took shape in his mind.

Day Ten, Year One, A. N. E.

A.N.E.: After the Nuclear Era. Why not? The future begins now; this is the first day of the rest of my life.

He licked the point of his lead pencil and began to write.

> *This is the journal of Evan Hale Mulligan, for the interest of historians and my descendants, if I have any.*

Evan rubbed out the last phrase with the eraser on the end of his pencil. Sounds too much like self-pity, he thought. I've got plenty to be thankful for.

He began a new paragraph:

> *The Third World War appears to be over. The nuclear component wrought terrible destruction, but it would have been much worse if not for the deterioration of metal alloys. The inexplicable phenomenon drastically reduced the munitions of both sides. Many of the major cities in America have been badly damaged, as has the infrastructure, and our enemies have suffered a similar fate, but the shortage of metal has forced a temporary and perhaps even permanent halt to the conflict.*
>
> *The Change we once thought might be the end of civilization has saved us.*

I am one of a group of survivors living on the farm of Edgar Tilbury, a man of foresight who anticipated the war and prepared for it. What Edgar didn't anticipate, what none of us anticipated, is what we would do when the war ended. In a way we are facing the end of all things. Look at it another way and we are at a beginning, like our distant ancestors at the arrival of the Ice Age. There is no way to escape, we have to stand and face it.

"Or go to Mars," Evan said aloud.

"What about Mars?" Lila Ragland leaned over Evan's shoulder. He hastily covered the words on the paper with his forearm. "Writing a journal, huh?"

"There's nothing wrong with that."

"Of course not, Evan, I was a journalist myself when we still had *The Sycamore Seed*. Do you want to be a writer? I thought you were going to be a vet, like Shay."

"I'm not sure."

"What was that you said about Mars?"

"Actually I was thinking about Mars Settlement. Since I was a little kid I've collected everything written about it, even really old issues of *National Geographic*. Sooner or later the human race is going to have to find another place to live; that's why there's so much interest in Mars.

"Our politicians can't see much beyond this afternoon; they want to spend our tax money where it'll do the most good for them personally. They don't care about space, it doesn't have enough voters in it." Evan paused; drew a deep breath; plunged ahead. "I'm thinking about a career in public service, Lila. I'd like to be remembered as one of the first statesmen on Mars."

"Whoa, there!" she laughed, widening her eyes. "Have you checked lately to see if it's dry behind your ears? That's a tall order for a young man."

"I know, but it doesn't scare me. Some of my ancestors went west in a covered wagon."

"At least their feet were on the ground," she said. "But let's go back to the subject of Mars. Why have a settlement there in the first place? Why not the moon? It's a lot nearer. I realize there was a certain romance in the idea of colonizing Mars, but that was when we had adequate resources for it; we weren't fighting a world war. Now it's a frivolous expenditure for bragging rights to a bauble millions of miles away."

"Mars is no bauble, Lila. It's the nearest planet to ours, it's within our reach, and it has some of the elements needed to sustain human life."

"Only with a big and expensive helping hand from us," she pointed out.

"Granted, but we can develop it in time. In the beginning Earth was no more than barren rock with an iron core, and a warm soup of minerals bathed by energy from the sun. When that mixture was struck by meteors that carried amino acids and proteins, the combination formed the first microbial life. It flourished here because the planet had water.

"Probes in the last century indicated that Mars was a similar situation. The moon has nothing in common with us; any colony there would have to live a totally artificial life. Mars has an atmosphere—thin, but it has one—and seasonal changes, polar caps, even volcanoes. Because it's a smaller planet it has less gravity than Earth, but a Martian day is almost the same length of time as ours."

A smile spread across Evan's face. "In a way, Mars Settlement will be like coming home and starting over. Maybe getting it right this time.

"And I want to be part of it."

10

Gloria knew that Kirby was troubled. He was a moody young man; his teenage years had exacerbated his volatility. She did not ask him what was bothering him because he resented personal questions. Instead she waited for him to come to her, which he did.

One evening he found Gloria alone in the living room, leafing through an old magazine of interior designs. The beautifully staged color photographs reflected a different time and the styles they depicted were outdated, but she found a certain comfort in looking at them.

This is how we were.

When Kirby sat down beside her on the couch, she smiled at him. He did not return the smile. "Jess Bennett never gives me a second glance," he said, "and I'm crazy about her."

"I know you are. She probably knows it too, but you can't make anyone like you; that's up to her."

"It's my face. I'll never attract any woman with this face."

"Forget about your face, you have a lot of the other qualities that women like."

Kirby shook his head. "I'm a monster." This was the first

time he had ever said it out loud; it was almost a relief. "Beauty and the beast."

"By the end of the story Beauty loved the beast," Gloria reminded him.

"She won't love me. As long as Evan Mulligan's alive Jess will never love me."

Gloria was used to Kirby's theatrics. "Don't talk nonsense," she said briskly. "We're going to have plastic surgery for you when it's available again. Then . . ."

"Then, nothing! That will be years from now and cost a fortune. Meanwhile Jess and Evan will get married. I've lost her, all right."

Gloria was tempted to say, "You never had her," but decided against it.

Bea Tilbury had become the shoulder everyone cried on. "Kirby's getting more and more depressed," Gloria told the older woman as they sat in the kitchen, drinking coffee and sharing gingerbread Bea had made. "Life's dealt him some bad blows and I can't reach him. His face is the mask he hides behind."

"I'd be surprised if he didn't. As for the plastic surgery . . ."

"I've made inquiries; the nearest reconstructive surgeon is in Madison and has a waiting list already. Kirby's right, it would cost a fortune we don't have."

Bea got up to refill their cups. Stirring hers, she said disdainfully, "Powdered milk. I'm sick to my back teeth of powdered milk, and powdered eggs have ruined my gingerbread."

"It's not ruined, it's just soggy in the middle, but it tastes fine. You should be glad Edgar stocked the ingredients."

"Oh, I am; he was a great one for planning ahead. Did you know he left me everything?"

"He loved you very much, Bea."

"And I loved him; loved him for himself. He could be an irascible old coot, but for me that was part of his appeal. We were so lucky to find each other at a time of life when many people have no one at all.

"I didn't know he was rich until after we married. Lila Ragland worked for him, you know; she handled his accounts and investments and certainly multiplied his wealth. In addition to this place, he owned other properties and a large portfolio of stocks and shares, and had bank accounts both here and abroad. One of his favorite sayings was 'Don't keep all your eggs in one basket.'" Bea smiled reminiscently. "He told me to be sure to remember that one.

"Edgar's fortune may have been diminished by the war, but I also had a legacy from O. M. Staunton, the president of the bank where I worked for most of my adult life. O. M. left the money to me with instructions—and these were his exact words—'Make the best possible use of this.'"

Bea took a bite of gingerbread and made a disapproving face. "Ugh. No matter what you say, this isn't up to my standard." She tipped her plate into the garbage can under the sink and turned back toward Gloria. "Now," she said in her most businesslike, president-of-the-bank voice, "What would you think of rebuilding the hospital in Sycamore River and calling it the Edgar Tilbury Memorial Hospital?"

Gloria set her cup down so hard the coffee sloshed out. "You mean it, Bea?"

"I'm always serious when I talk about money. I hope to find a first-rate plastic surgeon to join the staff, but even if I don't you can tell Kirby he's not going to have to wait for his surgery. Repairing his face is right at the top of my To-Do list."

When Gloria told her husband, Gerry drew back and stared at her in astonishment. "*How* much money?"

"Bea didn't go into details but it must be a lot. Even if Edgar took a hit because of the war, there was plenty left; she said he had money all over."

"I wouldn't tell Kirby anything about it, Muffin, until the money is actually available and a surgeon's agreed to have a look at him."

Meanwhile Bea Tilbury was thinking about that money. Word games. Riddles. Eggs in one basket . . .

She asked Jack, "When you collected those supplies from the shelter did you happen to see any boxes labeled 'Eggs'?"

"Eggs? No, I don't think . . . wait a minute. At the rear of the farthest tunnel there were some crates of eggs. We didn't bring them, we thought they were probably rotten by now."

"*Crates* of eggs?"

"Yeah, Aunt Bea; three or four."

"Dear God."

"What's the matter?"

"I want you to take me down there, right now."

"You don't want to go into that tunnel, Aunt Bea. It's dark and filthy and you might fall and break something. You're no spring chicken, you know."

"I'll tell you what I know: the next person who says that to me is going to get a kick in the shins!"

"Okay, but . . ."

"Are they wooden crates?"

"They are."

"Then bring a hammer, a pry bar and a big flashlight, and ask Gerry to help us."

"I don't see . . ."

"You may soon enough," Bea said.

The day was another one of oppressive heat. The gentle climb up the hill to the barn left her soaked in perspiration. Jack's disapproval did not make it any easier, but Gerry was as courteous as always. "Take my arm," he invited. "My wife told me about your wanting to rebuild the hospital. It's a great idea, Bea, but you'll be taking on a big headache; the main building is only a shell and the wings aren't much better. It could take a long time to find enough contractors to do the work. Every man who can drive a nail is going to be kept busy for years and years."

"I'm sure you're right, but money talks," Bea said.

"It will have to shout from the rooftops to get any special attention now. By the way, we're not going to tell Kirby about any of this yet. If we did and then something went wrong there'd be hell to pay."

When they entered the barn the horses nickered a welcome. Evan had begun keeping all four inside during the heat of the day. As Bea descended the steps to the tunnels she could feel cooler air. "That's better," she breathed gratefully.

Jack switched on his flashlight near the bottom of the steps. Edgar had electrified the shelter but turned everything off when they left. The unlit tunnels contained an almost tangible darkness. "Watch where you're going," Jack said. "There's plenty of evidence that we had dogs and cats down here." He aimed the flashlight beam to show what he meant. "Dogs anyway; the cats must have found a place to bury their droppings."

"They're a lot cleaner than dogs," said Bea. "I thought you knew that."

"I should, I've heard you say it enough times."

The tunnel farthest from the steps was not only dark but pungent with the remembered smell of earth. The flashlight beam revealed four wooden crates stacked, two by two, at the rear of the tunnel.

On the front of each crate was pasted a plain white label that read simply EGGS. Bea recognized Edgar's spidery handwriting.

Jack propped the flashlight at an angle that would illumine

the crates while he and Gerry lifted the first one down. "Damn it to hell, that's heavier than I thought! What kind of eggs are these anyway?"

Bea stepped close to watch while they pried off the lid.

She gasped.

11

"Is that what I think it is?"

"It's gold, Aunt Bea!" Jack was stunned. "Gold bars! Ingots. There must be a fortune here."

"It's Edgar's fortune; those are the eggs he didn't put in just one basket."

Gerry said admiringly, "That wily old fox."

The three stood in the bowels of the earth gazing down at gleaming beauty taken from the bowels of the earth.

"How much do you think there is?"

"I wouldn't even hazard a guess, Aunt Bea, but if the rest of the crates are like this one . . . we'll need to get one of these ingots assayed and multiply it accordingly. Better do it on the quiet, we wouldn't want to announce this to the public at large. You'd be asking to be robbed."

"Would you know where to get the gold assayed? For that matter, would you know how to convert it into spendable cash?"

Jack lifted one eyebrow. "This is me you're talking to. I could arrange it with no questions asked, which would be the smartest thing to do."

"When you were flying all over the world making deals for

people like Robert Bennett I never asked you to be specific about what you were doing. Maybe I was afraid it wasn't strictly legal."

His face was impassive. "I've always thought of you as a pillar of probity. Do you want to know now?"

Bea hesitated. "I want to know . . . if this much gold will rebuild the hospital in Sycamore River."

Jack laughed. "With this much gold we could almost build another Mayo Clinic."

"What about taxes? This is a huge inheritance, I'm going to owe a massive amount to Uncle Sam. I've already paid a lot on the money Mr. Staunton left me, but this will . . ."

Jack raised an eyebrow. "One step at a time."

That evening he told Nell, "I'm the nephew of a multimillionaire. I mean heiress. Aunt Bea would make Robert Bennett look like a pauper. Who knew?"

"Obviously no one did . . . except Lila. She must have. I'm surprised she didn't tie Edgar hand and foot and drag him to the altar."

"I thought you liked Lila."

"I do, but we're friends at arm's length. I know her type, they used to prowl around Rob. If I thought she was prowling around you . . ."

"No worries there," Jack assured his wife. "I already have a girl who fits my specifications exactly and her name is Nell Reece."

He then proceeded to demonstrate what a perfect fit she was.

The unrelenting heat grew worse day by day. On the rare occasions when any rain fell it was only a begrudging shower that lasted four or five minutes, evaporating as soon as it hit the ground.

Bea longingly recalled the coolness of the tunnels. Edgar's bolt-hole had sheltered them from more than bombs; it had maintained a temperate atmosphere. His house was airconditioned but the system had been installed years before, in a time of more salubrious weather.

"First plastic melted, then metal alloys, and now I'm melting," Bea complained at breakfast one morning.

"The Change only affected inert matter," said Jack. "It can't harm people."

"It's harming me, my heart's racing. If I'm out in the sun for only a few minutes I feel like I'm going to faint."

"Then don't go out in the sun," Gloria suggested.

"But I've always loved the sun, I used to have a golden tan for six months of the year. Now I'm developing a love/hate relationship with it."

"It's more than just a star, Aunt Bea, it's Earth's engine, and like most engines it can be used constructively or destructively. The moon has an effect on the tides, but the sun affects all life on Earth. Our ancient ancestors worshiped the sun instinctively; they never realized the complexity of its relationship with this planet. For a long time the human learning curve was very slow. Over two thousand years ago astronomers in Babylon discovered how to predict solar eclipses, but they didn't know how to use an eclipse to glimpse the solar corona."

Flub said, "Is that important?"

"For us it is. The solar corona is the sun's outer atmosphere. Electrically charged plasma is rare on Earth but most of the stars in the universe are made from plasma, which is a naturally occurring gas of positive ions and free electrons. Nano flares of plasma impelled by magnetic fields heat the sun's corona to many times the temperature of the sun itself. They're also responsible for the solar storms that disrupt radio waves and cause electrical outages on Earth. Are you following me so far, Aunt Bea?"

She gave a tiny start. She had been listening to a different voice; that of a university lecturer with gray eyes. "I'm right with you," she assured Jack.

"Okay. Because of its heat the solar corona continuously evaporates, producing an outflow of electrically charged particles we call the solar wind, which extends beyond the vicinity of Earth. When it encounters Earth's magnetic field the shock wave affects terrestrial air currents. A satellite designed to track the course of these currents was launched in Europe back in 2018, and within a few years every developed country had satellites of their own. Meteorologists were able to give extremely accurate forecasts of hurricanes, thunderstorms and tornadoes; all the dangerous weather events. Even the space program relied on that information. Since the dawn of time people complained about the weather. Now they could do something about it; they could save millions of lives.

"It sounded too good to be true and it was. When the Change struck, the satellites and most of the scientific equipment needed to operate them were lost. First plastic, then metal. A few items seemed impervious, but programs like our space agency had to practically rebuild. Developing replacements for compound metals has required a whole new technology, and it's ongoing. It may be another century before we get back to where we were."

"Whew!" whistled one of the twins. "Where'd you learn all that?"

"In school, Dub."

"I hate school. Me and Flub hate school; we wasted years and years there and we're glad it got bombed."

Jack absorbed this information without the slightest change of expression. He did not even raise an eyebrow. "The more fool you, then. If you're happy to spend the rest of your life sitting on a cold hard sidewalk, begging strangers to put coins in a paper cup so you can get something to eat, that's your business."

"Hey, wait a minute, I didn't say that!"

"It's the decision you're making right now." Looking across the table at Gloria, Jack gave her an almost imperceptible wink. "When I was your age I realized I needed an education to get what I wanted out of life, so I made a decision too. My real education began in the front row, third seat in of Mrs. Henry's science class. When she explained that theoretical physics seeks a single set of rules that apply to both the cosmic and the atomic scale, she started me on a voyage of discovery that . . ." Jack abruptly turned toward Lila. "Have you heard anything on the shortwave about the weather satellites? By some miracle are any still working?"

"I haven't been listening for information about satellites."

"But it's important, dammit! In terms of destructive power one EF5 tornado would be the equivalent of the atom bomb that was dropped on Nagasaki."

"Did an EF5 ever hit an American city?"

"I don't know, but . . ."

"I thought you knew everything, Jack Reece."

The twins cackled with laughter.

"I don't know everything," Jack replied in measured tones, "but I am aware we've been living in each other's pockets for too long."

That evening he had a suggestion for Nell. "The Bennett mansion is a ruin but Aunt Bea's house is as solid as the day it was built. No one's living there now. Would you like to have it?"

"Rent it, you mean?"

"Or buy it. Keep it in the family. What do you say?"

Nell and Bea were good friends in spite of thirty years' difference in their ages; their families had been friends for generations. Nell had visited so often that Bea's house felt like home. Contented cats curled in every soft chair, a sunny kitchen smelled of something delicious baking in the oven.

And Jack's old rubber tire, worn ragged, hung from a tree in the backyard.

She would be acquiring part of his childhood.

Nell's eyes danced. "I think we should buy it."

When they approached Bea to make an offer on her house, she was speechless.

Jack took her silence for disapproval. "It's a really good offer, Aunt Bea; we'll add another thirty thousand for the furniture and fixtures. I love the place and Nell does too. And of course you have Edgar's house."

"Of course," Bea echoed faintly.

She could not refuse without explaining why.

She could not bring herself to say, I don't want to spend the rest of my life with Veronica in her grave on the hill above me. Gloating over me.

I shouldn't think of her that way.

But I can't help it.

Maybe I'm just getting old.

I don't want to be old; really old. I'm not ready.

She felt a wash of fear. *I'm not ready.*

Before she went to bed she painstakingly counted the number of sleeping pills in the brown glass bottle she kept in the bathroom medicine cabinet. After Edgar's death she had complained of being unable to sleep. A doctor from Sycamore River had given her a prescription.

"Just take two, Beatrice, and only for as long as you really need them."

She was insulted. "Do you think I'm likely to become an opioid addict at my age?"

"I think they can creep up on you," he had warned.

Jack and Nell's offer for her house was discussed at length while dinner cooled on the dining table. The group had never thought of itself as a democracy and no votes were ever taken, but like a congenial family, every member was free to express a view.

Gerry said, "It sounds eminently practical to me. Bea won't have to worry about what strangers might do to her property, and you two will be getting a fine, solid house; they don't build 'em like that anymore—to coin a phrase. I don't suppose there'll be a mortgage?"

"The house will be a gift from me," Bea said stiffly. "To keep it in the family."

"Aunt Bea, you must let us pay . . ."

"A gift is a gift, Jack, and I mean it. If Finbar O'Mahony's still alive I'll have him draw up the necessary papers."

"Finbar's been the Bennett family lawyer for years," said Nell. "Having him represent you in this would be a conflict of interest, wouldn't it?"

Bea gave a dismissive wave of her hand. Behind the gold-rimmed spectacles she was thinking hard. Would there be a substantial tax difference between giving a gift to a nephew and giving your house to your son?

She almost laughed out loud.

I'll have enough money to pave the town, why am I worrying?

"With a big chunk of America in ruins, we're a long way from sorting out legal niceties," said Jack. "By the time it becomes necessary . . . Hell, Aunt Bea, we could all be dead by then." He grinned wolfishly. "Arrange this whatever way you like, and in the meantime if you agree to let us have the house, Nell and I can start moving our things over tomorrow. I'll bet the rest of you will be glad for a little more room here."

Looking slightly embarrassed, Shay Mulligan said, "I've been thinking about going home myself—Evan and Lila and me, that is,—if we wouldn't look like rats leaving a sinking ship."

Gloria turned to her husband. "You told me our new bedroom wing was demolished."

"'Fraid so, Muffin."

"Is there enough space for all of us in the rest of the house?"

"That depends on how willing you are to be cramped."

"We have plenty of room here and we were as cramped as sardines in the shelter; I can adjust either way."

A glance at Kirby convinced Gloria he would not like being cramped, and was prepared to make an issue of it. She said, "It might be best to stay here until we find a builder for the house."

Under his breath Jack repeated, "We could all be dead by then."

For many years the New England saltbox had borne a black sign identifying O'MAHONY, QUIMPER AND O'MAHONY, AT-TORNEYS AT LAW in gold letters. The house had been reduced to smashed clapboard and ashes. Atop the rubble the lawyers' shingle perched at a jaunty angle. Undamaged.

A fussy little man in shirtsleeves was poking at the ashes with a garden rake. The jacket of his suit was draped over the skeletal remnant of a dead rosebush; his white shirt was soaked with sweat. His concentration was so focused on what he might discover in the ashes that he never heard the pony and trap pull up behind him.

"Finbar O'Mahony! You're still alive."

He dropped the rake and turned around with a broad smile. "Bea Fontaine! You're right, to the best of my knowledge I am still alive."

"It's Bea Tilbury now; would you believe it?" she asked as Evan helped her out of the cart. She was carrying a large handbag and an even larger briefcase. "A brave man finally took me off the shelf."

Still smiling, the lawyer responded, "And here was me planning to do that one of these days. Would the lucky man be the Edgar Tilbury who founded that big engineering firm?"

"He would. Was; Edgar died recently."

"I'm so sorry."

"Thank you; I am too. It's part of the reason I'm here."

"Sadly, we can't talk in my office, Bea. What you see is all that's left; my shingle and that bench over there."

"At least you'll still have them when you open a new office."

O'Mahoney shook his balding head. "I don't plan to, it's time I retired anyway. I have a cabin up at the lake where I go to drown worms. That'll be the end of the firm; my father died years ago and Omar Quimper ran off with the receptionist." As he lifted his jacket off the ruined bush he said to Evan, "Why don't you get your horse some water while I talk business with Miss . . . Mrs. Tilbury? There's a spigot and pail around back."

He accompanied Bea to the bench and spread his jacket over the seat. "You mustn't get ashes on that pretty dress. Sit here and tell me what I can do for you."

She handed him the briefcase. "Edgar's will is in here; you'll see he named me as his executrix. He left everything to me except for a legacy to Lila Ragland. She worked for him at one time."

"That sounds straightforward enough. How much is 'everything'?"

"You'd better sit down by me."

As he looked through the papers and deeds the lawyer made small inarticulate noises. They reached a crescendo by the time he came to the end. "How the hell did he . . . I mean . . . this is a fortune, Bea!"

"And that's not all of it. He left me four crates of solid gold bars."

It was the first time in Bea's life that she had seen someone's jaw actually drop.

12

"I wish you'd seen the look on Finbar's face," Bea told Jack and Nell later.

Jack was amused. "A crusty old lawyer like that must think he's heard everything. A surprise was good for him."

"More than a surprise; for a minute I was afraid the shock might kill him. Evan had to give him some water from the horse's pail. We spent the whole afternoon going through paperwork. Finbar's going to handle the transfer of my house to you and Nell, but Edgar's affairs are much more complicated. The county courthouse and hall of records took a direct hit during the war, so . . ."

"Déjà vu," said Nell.

"What do you mean?"

"When RobBenn burned and the Nyeberger boys were injured, although they had caused the fire Dwayne Nyeberger tried to sue me for compensation. But the Change had done so much damage to the internet that retrieving the necessary records from the Cloud was impossible. The lawsuit was dropped."

"That's when you started believing in silver linings," Jack guessed.

Nell smiled and nodded.

Bea went on, "The situation with Edgar's will would not be so complicated if not for those gold bars. I explained to him that you, ah, knew people who would give you hard cash for them, but he seemed to think the whole idea was dodgy."

"In ordinary times I'd agree with him," said Jack, "but these are far from ordinary times. Immediately after a war things are done that wouldn't bear scrutiny later."

"I don't want you breaking any laws for me, Jack."

He gave Bea a look of such wide-eyed innocence she almost laughed. "Would I ever?"

Gerry Delmonico took his family to see what was left of their house. First he described the damage in some detail so there would be no unpleasant surprises, but when she saw it Gloria burst into tears anyway.

Kirby's reaction was troubling. The side of his face that could register emotion remained impassive. He might have been looking at a rock in the road. All he said was, "So what?"

"We're going to rebuild this wing better than before," Gerry assured him.

"Why bother?"

"It's our *home*, Kirby."

"Not my home. I don't have a home."

Gloria's eyes opened wide. "What are you talking about?"

"The Change. It happened before and it will happen again;

it destroys everything. I sure got changed, didn't I? Don't make such a big deal over a stupid house. Tear the rest of it down and sow the earth with salt, I don't care."

"I trained as a psychologist," Gloria said to Gerry later, "but I don't know how to help Kirby. It's impossible to reach him, he goes deep down into some dark place where nothing can touch him. I don't know what he's thinking down there or what he's capable of doing."

"He's a good kid at heart, Muffin, you know that."

"I don't know any such thing. Maybe we did wrong in adopting him, he needs more than we can give."

"The other boys are all right. Once they got used to living in a normal family, Buster and the twins fitted right in."

She would not be comforted. "I'm not worried about them, but I'm terribly worried about Kirby."

He watched her.

Kirby watched Jess constantly but she did not know.

The burns to his face had not damaged his eyes because he had closed them reflexively at the moment of the explosion, but a twisted ridge of skin ran down his face beside his left eye. The effect was curiously like a horse's blinkers. He had learned to tilt his head at an angle that allowed him to peer around the raised skin without revealing the eye.

There were unsuspected benefits to being a monster.

When tactful people were careful not to stare at him, it was almost like being invisible.

Jess did not stare. But wherever she was, Kirby was not far away.

Lila Ragland had been surprised to learn that Edgar had left her a legacy. She did not need it.

She had left her hometown of Sycamore River to escape the burden of a mother who was a notorious prostitute. In New York City she had discovered an intuitive genius for the computer. As a hacker she could uncover personal secrets and financial data sufficient to bankrupt billionaires and bring down foreign governments. With ten talented fingers she could siphon money out of any account that was not adequately protected. In a single day she could transfer a fortune to an offshore account, exchange it for dollars or any currency she chose, then transfer it again and again until it was untraceable.

Edgar Tilbury, who was old enough to be her grandfather, was the first man she had ever really trusted. When Lila returned to Sycamore River after her mother's death, he had become a mentor to her. To him she had revealed her success at cyber crime. Edgar had persuaded her it would be just as rewarding, and safer, to use her talents legitimately. "If it's the adrenaline rush that attracts you, come to work for me and help grow my investments."

Edgar had been right in his analysis of her character. The bulging portfolio of stocks and bonds that Bea had showed to Finbar O'Mahony was due in part to the efforts of Lila Ragland.

And now he was gone.

Lila did not know how to handle her grief.

When she and Shay became lovers they had exchanged intimate details, but she had given him a highly edited version of her earlier life. She was not the woman she had been; she did not think he would love that woman. It bothered her; she felt she was taking advantage of his trust.

If Edgar were still alive she could talk to him about it. He was a person you could tell anything. His absence was like a hole in the universe.

The offensive heat grew worse. Day by day the temperature crept higher, both in America and around the globe, as carbon emissions continued to pollute the atmosphere. Burning coal was the major source, but transportation played a substantial part as well. Those who were responsible fiercely defended their right "to provide jobs." The millions who had those jobs were paying a terrible price they did not realize.

An awful war had been fought, won and lost, yet war itself was not over. The abnormal heat drove people to random acts of violence they would not have undertaken in gentler weather.

Shamrock was an Irish setter, a hunting dog, an outdoor dog to the tip of his plumy tail. He had hated living in a bomb shelter and he hated being confined to a house. To keep the animals inside the bottom halves of the casement windows were always closed, but the heat necessitated leaving the tops partially open.

"Partially" was good enough for an athletic dog like Rocky. A leap and a scramble when no one was around, and he was on his way to freedom.

Late one evening he crawled home with a shoulder full of buckshot.

Jess was livid. While Shay painstakingly removed the pellets with a pair of eyebrow tweezers, she kept saying, "What kind of person would do something like that to a sweet dog? If I could get my hands on that monster I'd . . . I'd . . . do to him what he did to Rocky!"

That afternoon Kirby had seen two men hunting rabbits in the tall grass beyond the cattle guard. He also knew where Edgar's shotgun was kept.

13

In the wake of the war law enforcement was sparse. Those who had survived the combat were not eager to take part in another one. The Tilbury farm was outside the precincts of an urban police force, so when the doorbell rang, Bea was surprised to find a uniformed officer standing there. Red-faced and sweating profusely, he took off his hat and held it in his hands. "I'm sorry to bother you, ma'am, but are you alone out here?"

Bea's heart went out to him. He was young and obviously nervous, and trying not to show it. "Several people share this house with me, Officer. Is there a problem?"

He hesitated, reluctant to upset her. "It's, uh, a possible murder investigation."

"Murder?" she asked incredulously.

"Well, maybe; that's what we're trying to find out. Two brothers who live a couple of miles from here on the road to Hackett's Pond . . ."

"You must mean the Chalmers brothers."

"That's right; they were found dead under suspicious circumstances. We're talking to everybody in the area in case they know anything about it. I'm Detective Leon Sparks, by the way; I have my identification right here. . . ."

As he fumbled in his pocket Bea unlatched the screen door and held it open. "You're roasting alive out there, young man. Come inside and have some iced tea while we talk."

When the policeman stepped out of the glaring light it took time for his eyes to adjust. He stumbled against an umbrella stand before he saw it. "Sorry," he said to the stand.

Bea led him to the kitchen and had him sit down on a chair while she took a pitcher of iced tea from the refrigerator. During the moment the door of the appliance was open he felt a welcome wave of cool air.

Sparks drained two glasses of tea in quick succession, then fished out an ice cube and rubbed it across his forehead. When Bea offered him some paper-thin lemon cookies on a porcelain plate he held up a hand in refusal. Hesitated. Helped himself to a handful. "Who lives here with you?" he asked around a mouth full of cookies.

"The Reeces, the Mulligans—but they're planning to move back to their own homes soon—and so are the Delmonicos."

"Are those the Delmonicos who have the horse-bus?"

"That's right. The bus and the horses are in the barn at the top of the hill. If you'll forgive my curiosity, Detective, how did you get out here?"

"Bicycle."

"In this heat?"

"Yes, ma'am."

"Please don't call me ma'am, it makes me feel a hundred years old. I prefer Mrs. Tilbury."

"Yes ma'am," he replied automatically. They both laughed.

Bea said, "If law and order is being restored civilization must be returning too."

"Well, an effort's being made. It's like we walked up to the edge of the cliff and scared ourselves. The leaders of the major powers hope to hold a summit meeting to discuss denuclearization."

"That's wonderful news!"

"Maybe. Talking's not doing."

"You sound like my late husband. Now have some more iced tea and tell me about the murder."

Dinner table conversation was lively that evening, divided between those who wanted to talk about the possible murder and those who wanted to discuss the possible summit.

Jack asked Bea, "Will they be meeting at the United Nations?"

"No, probably in Philadelphia. Detective Sparks told me the UN was taken out by ICBMs. Some people hate the very idea of peace."

Gloria said, "I don't believe that, Bea."

"It's true whether you believe it or not," Jack interjected. "Facts are funny that way; there's only one truth, no matter how many 'alternate truths' are suggested. The urge to destruction is part of our DNA. Life as we define it is based on cycles of composition and decomposition. We build up only to tear down, whether it's our heroes or our cities. Most people claim to want peace, but the most financial profit and greatest scientific advancements are made during times of war."

Philip Delmonico put his elbows on the table and leaned forward. "I don't understand what you mean about decomposition."

"Everything on Earth, you and me included, is composed of a number of elements. What's the opposite of 'composed'?"

"Decomposed, I guess."

"All of the elements that make life possible are born in the heart of a star," Jack told him. "You'll learn that if you study physics, Flub. A star dies from the outside in. It releases layer after layer of its elements until it's reduced to a core of pure iron. The force of gravity continues to compress this core. When the dead star explodes from irresistible pressure it becomes a supernova. The power of the explosion drives its components outward to create a nebula of dust and gases, and the heavy elements are formed by fusion. Thus new stars are made and new planets shaped. So you might say creation begins with decomposition."

The youngster's face lit with excitement. "Physics!"

Gloria told Jack, "I think you have a convert. You would have made a wonderful teacher."

He replied straight-faced, "I've made several wonderful teachers in my time."

When Nell kicked him under the table, he laughed.

"You still have to tell us about the murder," Kirby said.

"Murder-suicide, that's what the police are calling it right now," Bea replied, "but they're waiting for a detailed forensic report. According to those who knew them the two Chalmers brothers got along very well; they were amiable men with only a year's difference in their ages. It's hard to understand why they would batter each other to death; even harder to understand why, at the last minute, one would cut the other's throat. We think there might be a third party who made it look that way in order to rob them, but nothing was missing; there was still money in the house and in their wallets."

"Brothers fight dirtier than anybody else," observed Daniel Delmonico. "That's why civil wars are never civil."

"Detective Sparks thinks the heat may be at least partially responsible. He says that for every degree the thermometer goes up, so does the rate of violent crime. It has him pedaling all over the county in this awful weather."

Jack said, "It's a plausible theory, Aunt Bea. Heat makes us all short tempered. Maybe it's a variant on the Change; melt the people instead of plastic and metal."

"That's not remotely funny."

"I wasn't trying to be, I'm just looking for explanations."

"Stick with hard science," Gerry advised. "The answer's bound to be there."

Jack said, "The Chalmers case doesn't sound like it had much to do with any kind of science."

Nell plucked at his sleeve. "I can't breathe," she said in a faint voice.

"Would you like to lie down?"

"Maybe for a little while, Jack; I feel so foolish. . . ." But she let him carry her upstairs without further protest.

She's too light, he thought. She's too damned light, she's going to blow away from me.

He turned down the cover on the bed, their bed, and plumped the pillows for her. He waited at the door in case she wanted anything else, but she kicked off the sheet, closed her eyes and turned her back to him.

It was too hot for physical intimacy.

When Jack returned to the dining table Buster Delmonico, the quietest of the boys, was having a coughing fit. It sounded exactly like one of Nell's.

"Gloria . . . this chest infection or whatever-you-call-it that my wife has . . . is it contagious?"

"That depends on what's causing it, Jack. An infection can be either viral or bacterial."

"Sounds like your Buster might have it too."

She glanced across the table at him; a stocky, robust athlete two years younger than Kirby. "But he's never sick."

"This isn't like measles or mumps, it's entirely different. You heard Gerry's theory about the . . ."

"Gerry always has a theory. I love him to bits, but he's no doctor."

"I happen to think he could be right about the global atmosphere changing. Plastic and metal changed too, remember."

"I don't see any relationship between them and the air we breathe."

"Like Gerry says, everything on Earth is related," Jack replied. "We've never discovered the reason behind the Change; we're only sure there must have been one. Maybe the same reason applies to altering the atmosphere. If it does, and we don't find a way to stop it, we'll roast alive or smother to death. Either way, we're looking at an extinction event."

The people sitting around the table exchanged glances.

The room was very quiet.

Shay Mulligan cleared his throat. "If it's going to be the end of the world, maybe we won't go home after all. You're the people I'd rather die with."

The heat was relentless; the principal and sometimes the only topic of conversation. During lunch on a breathlessly hot afternoon Lila reported, "I just heard on the shortwave that this is the hottest summer in ninety years; especially in the Midwestern states. Most of Alaska is only a few degrees above normal."

"That's the first good news today," said Jack, pushing away the plate containing his uneaten sandwich. "Good for Anchorage and Juneau, I mean. Maybe we should move there. Cram all of us and our possessions and our dogs and our cats into the horse-bus and chase the weather around the continent.

"In the last century people did just that; they thought it was the height of luxury. As soon as they retired they bought an expensive motor home and filled the tank with expensive gas and drove all over America, seeing the sights. Burning up petroleum without a thought in the world. Some of those sights aren't worth seeing now. They've been blasted to hell."

"Is there a point to all this?" Shay wanted to know. He had learned to recognize the beginning of one of Jack's lectures. They were always interesting and often entertaining, but in the enervating heat he preferred silence.

"My point," Jack replied, "is simply this. The Change was global but our heat wave isn't. If ninety years ago the weather here was hotter, what we're experiencing is normal rather than unnatural."

"So it's not an extinction event?"

"Not unless a comet slams into us; that's what did for the dinosaurs. We're probably way overdue for that particular catastrophe."

"You have a dreadful sense of humor, Jack Reece!"

"You used to say you loved everything about me, Nell Reece."

She frowned at her husband. "There's an exception to every rule."

Just then the doorbell rang. Bea went to answer it and returned with Leon Sparks.

The young policeman had begun visiting the Tilbury farm whenever he could. He liked iced tea and he liked lemon cookies, but most of all he liked Bea Tilbury, who reminded him of his grandmother. If there was an unidentified killer still on the loose, he hoped his frequent presence would be a visible deterrent.

It was the first time Sparks had seen all the occupants of the house. They were seated around a dining table extended to its full length, augmented by a folding card table. Every face turned toward him. One of them was shockingly scarred, but his police training stood him in good stead. He did not react at all.

"My family," Bea said proudly. "Let me introduce you."

Sparks tried to memorize their names. He did well with the adults, but the younger Delmonicos presented a problem. When Bea said, "Buster," Gloria amended it to "Brewster." "Flub and Dub" were Philip and Daniel. "They have an older brother," Bea said, "but Sandy's away in the navy."

"Sanderson," Gloria corrected.

Leon Sparks was relieved to hear that Kirby was just Kirby. The young man with the dreadful scars kept his face turned away most of the time. Obviously he did not like people to look at him.

"Will you join us for lunch?" Bea invited. "It's only a cold salad, no one wants hot food these days."

"I already ate, thanks . . . but I wouldn't say no to a glass of iced tea." As he spoke, the policeman's eyes were drawn to the pretty young woman identified as Jessamyn Bennett.

Kirby turned then and looked directly at Leon Sparks. There was something in his expression that had nothing to do with his disfigurement, but was chilling.

14

Jack Reece asked, "Have you caught your murderer yet?"

"We're not sure of his identity; the person who was responsible may have escaped. Or it may be what it appears to be, a murder-suicide. The scene was like a slaughterhouse, with blood everywhere. There had been a terrific fight and . . ." The policeman's voice ground to a halt. He realized he was making the wrong impression on Jess Bennett. She was looking at him with revulsion.

"We're not supposed to discuss a crime under active investigation," Sparks said hastily. "That's why I'm here: to ask if any of you might have remembered something, anything, that could help us. Maybe something you forgot to tell me when I was here before." He looked from face to face. Nothing.

"That's the Chalmers brothers, right?" Kirby asked, forgetting to be careful about shaping his words.

He hisses like a snake, Sparks thought. "That's right, the Chalmers brothers. Did you know them?"

"We were acquainted but they didn't know me. Nobody wants to know me. Would you?"

Jess Bennett put one hand on Kirby's arm. "We all know you, Kirby, and we love you. Is there anything you can tell the police that might help them?"

Kirby looked down at his hands and began to pick at the cuticles. "I used to go over there sometimes. They had chickens in a pen, several hens and two cockerels—that's a young male chicken. They're called Silkies and they're a very special breed; fancy white birds with silky feathers. The Chalmers brothers took theirs to shows just for chickens. Afterward they'd hang the ribbons their birds had won on the side of the pen. If nobody was around I'd go in the pen and sit down and the Silkies would sit on my lap or my shoulders. I'm a big man but they weren't afraid of me; they let me stroke them because we're friends."

Kirby lifted his head and asked the policeman, "What's going to happen to those chickens, do you know? Do you suppose I could have them?"

"I don't know, Kirby, but I'll make some inquiries this afternoon."

When Bea accompanied the policeman to the door he asked in a low voice, "Is Kirby retarded?"

"Lord, no! He's very intelligent, he got top grades all the way through school. He was offered a full university scholarship but he wouldn't accept it. He's very reluctant to go out in public."

"But sitting on the ground petting chickens . . ."

"He's lonely," said Bea. "With that face he's never been able to make friends."

"I can understand."

"I doubt if anyone else can really understand," Bea replied, "but things are going to get better for him. Now that the war's over we're going to get the best plastic surgeon available to fix his face."

"Is it possible to do that?"

"I've looked into it; disfigurements much worse than Kirby's have been successfully repaired. It may take several operations and a lot of time spent in the hospital, but the results will be worth it. The surgeon says he may be a really handsome man. But don't mention the surgery to Kirby; we haven't discussed it with him yet. We don't want to get his hopes up until everything's in place. He can be, well, temperamental."

"Plastic surgery can be expensive," Sparks warned.

Bea smiled. "Let us worry about that."

As he rode his bicycle away from the farm, Leon Sparks was puzzling over three mysteries. The Tilbury property was well-kept and undoubtedly valuable, but nothing exceptional. Not like a millionaire's compound. Yet four families who appeared to have little in common were living together like a tribe.

One of the Chalmers brothers, who had appeared to be devoted to one another, might have slaughtered the other in a blind rage.

And a badly damaged young man had to sit on the ground and pet chickens in order to experience love.

"Do you think they'll let me have the Silkies?" Kirby asked Bea.

"I should think so; when a person dies their property usually goes into probate, but those chickens are alive and they'll need care right away. Someone's probably wondering what to do with them right now."

When he heard the news Shay was delighted. "Well done, Kirby. We're going to have our own fresh eggs!"

"Don't count your chickens before they arrive," Bea warned.

Arrive they did, two days later, crammed into a large wicker container precariously balanced on the luggage rack of Leon Sparks' bicycle. The chickens' squawks of outrage could be heard all the way from the cattle guard.

Kirby was overjoyed.

"Take your chickens up to the barn," Jack said, "and put them in there until you get a proper pen built for them. If you turn them loose outside one of the dogs will get them sooner or later."

"Not Samson, he's not fast enough with only three legs."

"Don't kid yourself, Kirby. Animals don't acknowledge handicaps, they just get on with their lives. Be sure to close the door to the bomb shelter; if those chickens get down into the tunnels we'll never find all of them. There's an old bicycle in the barn too; the Change damaged the handlebars but it's still usable. It should be covered with something other than chickenshit."

Building a pen for the Silkies became a priority.

With wood from the woodlot, Edgar's tools and Buster's help, the project was soon accomplished. The pen was placed next to the barn so the larger building would provide shade during the heat of the day. Kirby showed off what he called "The Chicken Palace" with pardonable pride.

Jess was on hand to watch the birds explore their new home. "I really enjoyed doing this," Kirby told her. "It's time I found a job for myself, and the country's going to need a hell of a lot of reconstruction. Maybe I could become a carpenter's apprentice. My scars wouldn't matter so much then."

"Your scars don't matter now," Jess said. "Besides, you're going to have plastic surgery."

"Oh sure I will, someday," he replied sarcastically. "I won't hold my breath. But . . . did you mean what you just said? About my scars?"

"Of course I did. When I look at you I don't see them, I just see Kirby."

After Jess went back to the house he felt something running down his cheek. He explored it with tentative fingertips.

He was crying.

Philip Delmonico was not interested in chickens, unless they were fried, and he could not imagine why Kirby was. He was probably up to something, Flub decided; Kirby was always up to something but no one ever blamed him. His dreadful injuries were giving him a free pass through life. When Edgar Tilbury died, Kirby had appropriated a lot of his books without asking permission and nobody complained.

What was in those books that Kirby wanted to keep for himself?

The distraction of the chickens gave Flub an opportunity to find out. When Kirby was preoccupied with the Silkies, Flub went to search his room.

The books were not there.

He stood in the middle of the room and slowly rotated. Bed, nightstand, chest, desk, chair, posters on the walls . . . no books. His eyes went back to the bed. Dropping to his hands and knees, Flub lifted the edge of the bedspread and peered underneath.

There they were. Stacks and stacks of books; Edgar Tilbury's lifelong collection of dictionaries and encyclopedias and volumes of research material completely filled up the space. All the reading material an inquiring mind could wish for.

Flub reached for the nearest book and pulled it out: a slim hardback entitled *Exploring the Space/Time Continuum.*

Physics?

He sat down on the bed and had just begun to read when, "What the fuck are you doing in my room?" Kirby demanded from the doorway.

Startled, Flub jumped up, dropping the book onto the floor. "I . . . I was just . . ."

"Snooping, that's what you were doing, you weasel." Kirby picked up the book and smoothed down a folded page. "What do you want with this? You wouldn't understand a word of it. I happen to know you hated science in school."

Flub held his ground. "Maybe I did, but a guy can change his mind, can't he? I keep thinking about the strange things that have happened, the melting plastic and the disintegrating metal and the awful weather that just gets worse and worse. It's like an itch in my brain, you know what I mean?"

Kirby nodded. "I know exactly what you mean."

"I figure there have to be reasons for all the crap. Maybe there's even one scientific explanation that covers everything."

"I guess that's possible, Flub, but I wouldn't have thought of looking for the answer in here." Kirby frowned at the book in his hand.

"Why not? Edgar was a smart man and he kept a lot of really scholarly stuff. Have you read this one yet?"

"Not yet, but . . . here, sit down by me and let's have a look."

"Just don't start at the beginning," Flub said. "Introductions are boring."

Kirby opened the book to a random page and read aloud: "'What we think of as gravity is actually the push and pull of time and space. Time and space are relative. Gravity and acceleration are the same.'" He stopped reading for a moment and stared into the distance. Then he resumed. "'Mass causes the curvature of space/time. Matter tells space and time to curve. Space and time tell matter to move.'"

He repeated the last two sentences very slowly. "'Matter tells space and time to curve. Space and time tell matter to move.'"

15

At dinner that evening they expected Kirby would talk about his chickens, but instead he entered the dining room with a book under his arm. He plopped it down on the table in front of Jack. "Open to page thirty-four," he said without preamble, "and read the text I've underlined."

Jack read the few lines, looked up at Kirby, then read them again. "There's nothing new here. This was taken from one of Albert Einstein's famous speeches at Princeton University, long before we were born. Why do you . . ."

Kirby said patiently, "Think about the Change."

"I still don't . . ." Jack read the text one more time, word for careful word. "Oh. Yes."

"You see it now?"

"I do, and I don't know how so many other people missed it. This passage is an esoteric description of a method by which plastic and metal can be . . ." Jack paused, searching for the right word. "Can be transmuted. Maybe it took fresh eyes to recognize it. How did you come across this?"

"By accident," said Flub.

"Or coincidence," Kirby amended. "Do you remember a

conversation some time back about composition and decomposition? This is an extension of that same train of thought. What was the Change but controlled decomposition?"

Gerry left his chair and bent over Jack's shoulder, reading avidly. "It could be," he muttered. "It just could be. But who . . . ?"

"That's the next mystery," Jack said. "Who knows enough about physics to maneuver atoms of plastic and metal into reconstituting themselves? And don't tell me it was aliens from another planet, Evan."

"I wasn't about to. It had to be some genius right here on Earth. Or more likely, a whole laboratory of geniuses; an updated version of Los Alamos."

"If it was the enemy we just fought a war against," Lila said, "why didn't they use their discovery to destroy us?"

"They didn't use it at all," Gerry replied. "They suffered from the Change just like we did. But America has more than one enemy. The next one may be waiting in the wings."

The heat continued.

"At least no one needs to weed the garden," Nell remarked to Bea one evening as a burning sun was sinking in a burning sky. "Most of the weeds are dying too. I'm glad you did so much canning before the fruit and vegetables shriveled up."

"We may have enough to last us through the winter if we're careful," said Bea, "but next year . . ."

Jack looked glum. "We may not have a winter this year. Check the calendar. We should be experiencing at least a ten percent drop in the nighttime temperature by now and there isn't any. If the summit of the great powers does meet in Philadelphia, the first item on the agenda should be the climate."

"That should have been the first item on the agenda a hundred years ago," Gloria said bitterly.

Kirby moved the Silkies' pen into the barn and left it there. The horses remained inside too, as they had done during the war. Jack and Shay rigged up a system of electric fans that kept the barn temperature almost tolerable, and the animals had fresh water constantly available.

When Edgar was looking for property in the country to buy, one of the factors that had made him decide on this farm was an unusually deep artesian well. The water had tested almost 100 percent pure. In spite of the sweltering heat on the surface, the water deep in the earth was cool.

Out of the well it soon warmed to blood temperature.

The air took on a faint scorched smell, as if something was burning at a great distance.

Bea's cats had always preferred to lounge in sunny windowsills, but the blazing sun was too much even for them. They did not want to stay in the house but scattered around the farm, seeking cooler sanctuaries. When Aphrodite failed to return for an evening meal, Bea was worried.

"It's not like her to miss a meal, Jack, that's why she's so fat."

"She's so fat because you had her neutered."

"The vet says that has nothing to do with it!"

Jack shrugged a nonchalant shoulder. "I bow to the expert. At least you can be sure Aphrodite hasn't run off with a passing tomcat."

"Take a flashlight and look for her, will you? I really am worried."

"Maybe a fox got her."

"Edgar said there aren't any foxes around here because they're too afraid of Samson. Edgar said a Rottweiler could eat a fox for breakfast."

Bea could hear herself: "Edgar said, Edgar said." *I sound like a new widow,* she thought.

I am a new widow.

She bit her lip and tried to think about something else.

In the stifling heat of the night Jack set out to look for Aphrodite. He went to every place that might harbor a cat, and some unlikely ones. During his years of experience with Bea's many felines he had learned to seek them where they could not possibly be. He combed through dying cabbages in the vegetable garden, pulled raspberry canes off the fence until he got thorns in his fingers, went to the woodlot and shone his light into trees destined for carpentry and hearth. No cat. She was not in the barn either—or if she was she refused to come when called.

At last he gave up and went home. As he got into bed he told Nell, "I felt like a damned fool stumbling around in the dark calling 'Kitty kitty kitty.' It's a shame cats don't come to a whistle."

"Cats and dogs hear in different ranges; they have almost nothing in common. Cats are not domesticated, no matter what their owners think. A cat is its own boss; maybe that's why some men don't like them. Every species has its own method for survival."

"What about Kirby's chickens?"

Nell laughed. "I don't know enough about chickens to comment, but I'll bet Kirby does. I'm just glad he's found a new interest, I was beginning to think his focus on Jess was . . ."

"Unhealthy?"

"Not exactly; maybe too healthy. I'd prefer for Jess to be involved with someone who doesn't have so many problems."

Jack stretched his long legs under the sheet, then tossed it aside. "Aside from his face, Kirby's okay. He certainly has an excellent mind; he got all the brains in the Nyeberger family."

"Do you think he's right about the Change?"

"I've been asking myself that ever since I read the passage in Edgar's book. People all over the world searched for an explanation. It defies all the odds that Kirby would stumble across it accidentally, and *recognize* it. How many thousands read those words and never saw what he did?"

"A lot of apples had to fall out of a lot of trees," said Nell, "before Sir Isaac Newton recognized gravity." She gave a sharp intake of breath when she felt his exploring hand. "Stay on your side of the bed, it's too hot for that. You'll make me cough again."

"That's it," Jack said flatly. "This heat's interfering with my love life and it's going to have to stop."

The heat did not stop. The temperature continued to climb upward by minute increments all day. Every day.

And every night, making sleep impossible for those who did not have air-conditioning.

The longed-for restoration of the national grid was painfully slow. The inexpensive and reliable combination of hydro power, solar panels and wind turbines that generated the nation's electricity had been vulnerable to targeted attack. Crews throughout the United States were working around the clock to make the necessary repairs.

Meanwhile the residents of Tilbury Farm used their generator and old-fashioned oil lamps. They even felt a bit smug about it. There was no more talk about moving back to their own houses, which were fading into memory. The farm answered all their needs. Life settled into a comfortable self-sufficiency.

—————

The calendar indicated autumn but there would be no autumn that year; no season of crisp mornings and multicolored leaves. On the overheated planet storm season came instead.

Hurricanes formed in the Atlantic in swift succession; giant beasts measured as category four and five . . . mostly five. They ravaged the eastern coast of the United States while their twins the typhoons attacked Hawaii, the Philippines and Hong Kong.

A few diehard Flat Earthers still insisted that climate change was all a hoax; their relatives considered committing them to a home for the seriously bewildered.

While Shay and Lila were sitting on "Veronica's balcony" one evening, hoping to catch the faintest breeze, they saw distant stars twinkling at ground level.

Lila shrieked, "Lights! *Lights,* Shay!"

"I don't believe it."

"Just look! They're in a straight line . . . that must be along the road east out of Nolan's Falls."

They were as enthralled as toddlers watching the lights on a Christmas tree. After a few moments Shay jumped to his feet. Hurrying inside, he shouted the news and began flipping light switches. People were answering him from different areas of the house. "Lights? Are you sure?"

"He's pulling your leg."

"He better not be. Did you actually see lights, Shay?"

"Honest to God, we could see them from the roof. Lila thinks they're on the road to the state capital; go up and look for yourselves."

There was a thunder of footsteps on the stairs.

16

Kirby was in a deepening depression.

Aside from feeding his chickens and supplying them twice a day with fresh water, he was no longer spending time with them. His usually healthy appetite dwindled to almost nothing, but he was doing a lot of reading. Some of the books were from Edgar's scientific collection. Others shone a light on human nature.

He had read *Frankenstein* only once and hated it, but he read *The Strange Case of Doctor Jekyll and Mister Hyde* over and over again, recognizing himself in Stevenson's psychological thriller; aware that he also stood on a knife edge between the good side and the bad side of his nature.

He remembered nothing of the explosion that had almost cost his life and left him badly disfigured. Memory had resumed with waking up in the hospital and seeing himself in a bathroom mirror. From that moment the anger had been building in him; throughout his childhood and his teenage years and on into manhood. Hatred for a world that conspired against him. He did his best to hide the rage which had become a cornerstone of his personality, but still it threatened to break through.

Occasionally he was able to step out of the shadow. When he found the Einstein quote and saw how applicable it was to the Change, other people had looked at him with admiration. That had been a shining day. So was every day when Jess Bennett smiled at him. He thought those might be the high point of his entire miserable life.

Gloria was aware of his increasing moodiness. "I'm going to tell Kirby about the plastic surgery," she said to Gerry. "I know we agreed not to, but it may be the very thing he needs most."

"It's hard to know anything for sure about him, Muffin. He keeps everything locked inside. I suspect he was doing that long before we adopted him."

"I'm sure he was, it may be too ingrained a habit to break. But it must have started with the explosion, so if we can undo the physical damage that caused he might have a chance for a normal life."

After supper she found Kirby on the back porch, sitting on the steps in the gathering twilight. Sitting alone, doing nothing. Staring into space.

She sat down beside him and after careful consideration, put one hand on his knee. Sometimes Kirby did not mind being touched; sometimes he did.

When he did not pull away she said gently, "There's something you need to know. It's not a hundred percent sure, so we've put off telling you, but . . ."

He did not look at her. "Something good? Or something bad?"

"Something very good, Kirby! Bea Tilbury has come into quite an amount of money."

"That's good for her, but what does it have to do with me?" He still stared into space.

"She's going to use it to rebuild the hospital in Sycamore River . . . and to pay the best plastic surgeon we can find to repair your face."

Kirby did not move; he did not respond.

When Gloria turned to look at him she saw his eyes were closed, like a man in a dream. And he was smiling.

He was going to have his own face back again. A wonderful new future opened out before him. He could hardly wait to tell Jess.

When the national grid went dead many people had left their useless light switches turned on, so they would know when, or if, the force came back. Almost every American would remember what he or she had been doing when the grid was restored. The epic moment when The Lights Came On. If they did not remember, it was because they were asleep, or drunk . . . or engaged in something extremely important.

When the flood of electric light washed over them, Jess and Evan had been in her bed. The door was closed and they had extinguished the oil lamp. Being invited to her room was a rare treat for Evan. He thought of them as lovers. She did not. They had sex rarely and only when she initiated it. The first time they were together he had thought she was a virgin, but he could not be sure. His sexual experience was limited; Jess was his first and only girl. She was good in bed but it felt like she was holding something back. Evan did not know if she was intimate with anyone else. From the beginning he had been certain she was the one for him, but he could not tell how she felt. When he questioned her she had a dozen elliptical answers, none of them satisfying.

"Do you know how much I love you, Jess?"

"As much as I love you, I suppose."

"How much is that?"

"You can't measure love, Evan. It might be a half teaspoon full or enough to fill a gallon jug."

"But you are going to marry me someday?"

"I'm too young."

"You are not, you're well over the legal age for marriage."

"Women don't think they have to get married these days, the way our grandmothers did." Jess was beginning to sound exasperated. "Marriage is for people who're ready to make a lifetime commitment and I don't know if I'll ever feel like that. I sure don't *now*."

If she was not willing to discuss marriage at some future time, how could he persuade her to go to Mars with him?

How could he go without her?

Evan knew only one thing to do. He was courting her subtly, but constantly, with a quiet desperation. This evening his persistence was about to be rewarded . . . until the penul-

timate moment, when someone jiggled the knob of her bedroom door.

At the same moment the overhead light came on.

"Jess? Are you in here?"

Evan was dismayed to hear Kirby's voice. He shouted,
"What the hell are you doing out there?"

Kirby flung open the bedroom door.

The naked couple on the bed pulled up the covers and
stared at him. They were illuminated by the electric light like
characters on a stage.

One heartbreaking glance told Kirby more than he wanted
to know. He spun around and ran from the room.

Jack intercepted him in the hall. "Hey there, where's the
fire?"

Kirby could not answer. He shook his head helplessly,
afraid he was going to vomit. Pushing the other man aside,
he ran on.

Jack started to go after Kirby, who had looked quite sick,
just as Jess came out into the hall. She was wrapped only in a
bedsheet. "Where did Kirby go?" she asked Jack.

"I don't know, he ran into me and went on. What's happened?"

"Something awful."

"The lights came on, Jess; there's nothing awful about that."

"Yes there is. Kirby opened my bedroom door and saw . . ."

"Us," Evan finished for her as he stepped into the hall. He
was fastening his jeans.

"You two were together?"

Evan nodded. "In bed." He was glad to confirm it; the fact gave substance to his love affair.

Jack Reece had not been aware of the emotional undercurrents of the younger generation on the farm, but the situation had just been dramatically demonstrated for him. He required only seconds to realize the ramifications. Kirby had seen the couple in bed and been tremendously upset. It must be because he was in love with Jess himself. Kirby was temperamental; his reactions were unpredictable.

"Get dressed, both of you, and go downstairs. Don't say anything about this to anyone until I find Kirby and have a chance to talk to him."

"What are you going to say to him?"

"I don't know, Evan; it'll depend on the state he's in, I guess."

This is just what I need, Jack was thinking. Every day seems to have its own problems, one step forward and two steps back. I thought when the war was over . . . well, no point in dwelling on it.

In order to find Kirby he went to Gloria. She and Gerry had been in their room when the lights came on, and they were bubbling with excitement until Jack explained what had happened.

Gloria in particular was distressed. "I knew he had a crush on that girl but . . ."

"I suspect it's more than a crush," Jack told her. "Kirby's reaction to the scene was pretty violent."

Gerry said, "He's not violent, remember how gentle he is with his chickens."

"Jess isn't a chicken, and I don't think he would hurt her anyway. But he might attack Evan."

"He wouldn't do any such thing."

"You didn't see the expression on his face; he looked like a different man. I want to find him and talk to him before he . . ." Jack left the thought unfinished. "Where does he go when he's upset, do you know?"

Gloria shook her head. "I have no idea. Kirby keeps himself to himself; particularly if he's upset."

"Gerry? You haven't seen him?"

"Not since supper, but we'll help you look for him. He must be somewhere on the farm."

Jack looked dubious. "Not too long ago I searched this entire farm for Aunt Bea's cat and never did find her."

By now it was dark; a sliver of crescent moon offered no illumination. They set out with flashlights to find Kirby. Gloria did not want to ask anyone else for help. "Kirby'd be mortified if the others knew."

"His embarrassment isn't my foremost concern at the moment," Jack told her.

They started with the barn. Jack was relieved to see that the four horses were still there, and so was Edgar's old bicycle with the sagging handlebars. "Maybe he's gone down to the shelter," Gerry suggested.

"No," said Gloria, "he hates the place."

They looked anyway, making their way through the maze of tunnels until they were convinced Kirby was not there. Then out into the night again: the meadows, the woodlot, the out-buildings, even the fields of neighboring farms . . . nothing. When Gloria was obviously exhausted Gerry insisted she go back to the house. Dawn found the two men standing alone on the back porch. "I'm stymied, Jack. Where the hell is he?"

"The ground didn't open up and swallow him, so he can't be too far away. Try not to worry, Kirby's a grown man, he can take care of himself."

Gerry's shoulders sagged. "You think so? I don't."

17

Kirby's disappearance came as a bombshell. At breakfast Jack gave the details as simply as possible. Even so, by the time he finished Jess was fighting back tears. "It's my fault, I didn't know he felt like that."

"You must have," Bea told her. "Women always know."

"But *Kirby*? Who would suspect that Kirby . . ."

"Because of his face? That's going to be fixed, Jess, and when it is he's going to be a good-looking man."

The others comforted Jess but no one had a kind word for Evan, who began to feel like the villain in the piece. He left the table before breakfast was over and went to the barn to saddle Rocket. He was just about to mount when Buster appeared. "I'm going to take care of Kirby's chickens until he comes back."

"You know anything about chickens?"

"Not a damned thing," Buster replied cheerfully. "But how hard can it be?"

"Everything in this world's hard," Evan told him with feeling. "Every single damned thing. Say, you want to go riding with me? You can have Juno, she's pretty calm. I'm going to go farther afield and see if I can find Kirby and bring him home; I'd like to be the hero instead of the villain."

As Buster saddled the gray mare he said, "I'd better warn you; when Kirby makes up his mind to do something he's mighty determined."

"So am I," said Evan.

As the lights returned from north to south, east to west, substation to substation, thankful Americans held Illumination Parties. They were brilliant.

The restoration of the national grid changed the face of the nation. Residential lighting was only a small portion of the demand for power. So much electricity was turned on at once that there were a number of temporary blackouts as cities and towns and farms, factories and office buildings and shopping centers gulped their share. So did uncounted millions of air conditioners. Every possible object in America, from roller coasters to toothbrushes, had been electrified.

The president of the United States declared "National Appreciate Electricity Week."

The utility companies promptly raised their charges.

Coincidentally, the heat wave broke all known records. Soon retailers not only were out of every model of air conditioner, they did not even have any electric fans.

As heavy industry went back into action the first jolt of industrially produced methane entered the atmosphere. No one complained; profits would begin rolling in again soon.

Nell Reece knew she was seriously ill but would not admit it. Jack already had too much on his plate. He was working very hard, as he put it, "to keep all the balls spinning." Life would have been easier for him if the other families had moved back to their own homes after they left the shelter, but the experience they had shared had affected them in an unexpected way. They preferred to remain together, an option made possible by the size of the Tilbury house.

Shay teasingly called them a "clan" and suggested they all adopt the same surname. "Mulligan would sound great," he said.

Gerry snorted with laughter. "Then I'd be a black Irishman!"

Jack had been the leader of the group, and when Edgar died, the role of patriarch became his too. Jack the adventurer, Jack the lone wolf, looked after everyone.

There were times when he asked himself how the hell *that* happened.

Bea kept the central air-conditioning in the house running all the time but it fought a losing battle against the unrelenting heat. Even the nights were insufferably hot. It was almost impossible to sleep; if someone did succeed they awoke with a splitting headache and drenched in sweat.

As Nell's illness grew worse Jack brought a portable air

conditioner from the tunnels and installed it in their room. Still, she could hardly breathe. Her skin was pale and clammy and she had no appetite.

Gloria said sternly, "You should be in the hospital."

"What hospital? Tilbury Memorial won't be ready for a couple of years and Nolan's Falls is just a maternity hospital. Unless I'm swelled out to here they won't let me in the door."

"I could go with you; I could explain how serious the need is."

"People all over the country are probably trying to buy or bluff their way into any hospitals that are still standing. Why should I get preference?"

"Nell, sometime you're too nice for your own good."

"I'm not. If you really knew me . . ."

"You're my friend and you're sick, that's all I need to know. Without expert medical care you're likely to get a lot sicker."

"What do you think the problem is?"

"I'm not an expert on thoracic diseases; I only learned enough biology to get a nursing certificate. But when I looked down your throat I didn't like what I saw. The surface is covered with tiny little blisters, somewhat like a bad sunburn."

"How could I get a sunburn in my throat? Standing in the sun all day with my mouth open?"

"I said somewhat *like,* Nell. Not the same as. If that's the condition of your throat lining the same thing may have happened to your lungs. We've already tried honey and cough syrup and expectorants but nothing worked. It's puzzling and it's serious and I think you need to see a specialist. One of the men could take you to the state capital and . . ."

"In the pony and trap? No thank you, Gloria; I couldn't stand it. Do you know how much my chest hurts?"

"That's why we have to . . ."

"No! Now stop going on about it."

"Talk to her, Jack," Gloria pleaded.

"It won't do any good, the word 'adamant' was invented for my wife."

He was more worried than Gloria, but he was aware that nagging Nell about the hospital would only make her more determined not to go. He pinned his hopes on her pain; when it hurt enough she would relent.

This was the contest he had dreaded; facing her possible mortality.

Kirby Delmonico was not worried about his mortality but he needed to find a way to get some money.

When he left the farm in a blind rage he had empty pockets. He had stalked away in the dark, fighting his demons, and kept walking until his temper eased; by then he had traveled several miles. He decided it was best to stay away for a while. If he saw Evan Mulligan he might do something he would regret.

Since he was accidentally headed in the direction of Nolan's Falls he went the rest of the way. It was a long walk but he was a healthy young man with good night vision. He strode along, swinging his arms and enjoying the power in his legs. As he walked he made plans. Kirby was not a proud man—with his face he could not afford pride—but he realized he had one asset.

At the edge of town he noticed an open garbage can with several discarded paper cups on top of the other rubbish. He selected the cleanest and carried it with him until he found a water faucet. When the cup was thoroughly rinsed he dried it on the tail of his shirt.

Dawn found him sitting in front of the bombed-out bus station, holding out his cup in a clawlike hand. As the morning progressed the cup began to fill with coins and dollar bills. Even a couple of fivers. Passersby would take one startled glance at his ruined face and quickly dig in their pockets.

When he had enough money to pay for a room he went to the nearest hotel. The clerk at the front desk gave him a quizzical look but asked no questions. Kirby said tersely, "Industrial accident."

"Fuck it, that's too bad. I hope you sued the bastards for everything they had."

"We tried, but their lawyer was better than our lawyer and the fix was in." Kirby enjoyed improvisations. "You can't beat the big guys."

"Naw, you sure can't beat the big guys. I could tell you some stories . . . Well, listen. You need anything while you're here, you just ring the desk, you hear? Anything at all."

Pity, Kirby said to himself with distaste. His ruined face was his asset; it was a hell of a world that had nothing better to offer him.

"Is there a public library in this town?" he asked the clerk.

"Sure; the Carnegie. Go out the front door, turn right, and it's two blocks down on your left."

"It hasn't been bombed?"

The clerk said, "Who'd target a library?"

Half of Kirby's mouth smiled. "Ideas are the most powerful weapons of all."

When he had been missing for five days Gloria feared the worst. "Gerry, do you think he's killed himself?"

"I doubt it, Kirby's not the type; he's never given in to self-pity. He'll come home when he's ready."

"Stop saying that. I've studied psychology, remember? Anyone might be suicidal if they're under enough stress. That friend of Bea's on the police force, Detective Sparks—I'm going to file a missing persons report with him."

"We recently went through a war, Muffin; as a result I'll bet there are quite a few missing persons. Leave it, will you?"

Leon Sparks told Gloria the same thing. "Plenty of guys go missing every year. Sometimes it's a family quarrel or a nasty row with the wife; as soon as he cools down, or she does, they get back together. Sometimes he moves out of state, changes his name and marries a different woman. There are a lot of reasons for a guy to drop off the radar screen. Wait a while and see what happens." Recalling Kirby's face, he thought suicide was a definite possibility, but he did not say that to her. "I'll put your son on our list and have a flyer printed. If you have a photo we could copy and . . ."

"We have no photo of him as he looks now," Gloria said sadly. "We wouldn't do that to Kirby."

After the policeman left the house Gloria sat in a chair on the back porch for a while. She very much needed to talk about Kirby, but Gerry wouldn't listen. Perhaps having Kirby as part of their family had been too much of a strain.

The day was far too warm. Any humidity had long since evaporated, leaving even the sturdy shrubs around the foundation of the house parched and dry. Gloria left the porch and went to have a closer look at them.

Dying; they who had been living. It was cruel.

She walked around the house, bending close to one plant after another. Breathing moist breath on the shriveling leaves. "Can you hear me?" she murmured. "Do you know you're dying? If I bring a couple of buckets of water to you, will you try to stay alive?"

18

Lila Ragland liked Nell; everyone in the house liked Nell. But Lila's affection was not straightforward. She was also jealous of her. Nell had Jack Reece, who was the most exciting man Lila had ever met.

What did a man like that see in Nell? Lila wondered. Granted, she was pretty in a blond, cookie-cutter sort of way, but surely Jack could do better.

What would he say if she undertook to seduce him?

Lila had faith in her skills as a seductress. Those skills had taken her from the slums on the wrong side of the Sycamore River into the beds of wealthy men who were more than willing to help her. Through them she had acquired a fashionable wardrobe, polished manners and an invaluable education. She had never loved any of the men who provided these things; she never loved anybody, though she was fond of Shay Mulligan. Having a prostitute for a mother had debased the concept of love for Lila. But if she could not love, she could desire.

And she desired Jack Reece.

As Nell's health deteriorated Gloria Delmonico was her nurse, but Lila became her companion. She read aloud to Nell, brought endless glasses of water and raised or lowered the window shades as requested. When Nell's scalp was wet with perspiration in spite of the air-conditioning, Lila washed her hair.

Any time Jack came into the room Lila was there, being attentive.

The repair of the national grid had meant electronic communications could resume. Wallscreens and radios came to life again, but during the interruption flaws had crept into the system. Components were individually owned and had not been maintained on a uniform level. Those who tried to get in touch with their loved ones by telephone frequently found the landlines jammed. Cell phones that relied on cell towers for transmission were not always reliable.

People told one another, "Everything used to work better," and complained about the static.

Meanwhile the relentless heat continued exacerbating medical conditions. Mounting death rates were reported in every state in the union. The very young and the very old were the most vulnerable, but males and females of every age fell victim to heat stroke or cardiac arrest.

Increased sighting of sharks and increased shark attacks were reported around the coasts of America. Ichthyologists believed the animals were being maddened by the increasing warmth of the sea.

Even when climate change was internationally recognized as an existential threat, politicians in the United States had been unwilling to support the necessary legislation to deal with it; they relied on the oil and coal industries for financial support.

Unlike the Chinese, they had missed their chance.

Now the damage was done. The long-threatened tipping point was approaching.

The planet was burning up.

The Andrew Carnegie Library in Nolan's Falls had excellent air-conditioning, thanks to the ongoing generosity of its long-dead benefactor. The library was considerably cooler than the hotel where Kirby was staying, so he spent most of the day in the reading room. The librarian, who reminded him of Bea Tilbury, kept classical music playing in the background at a low volume.

When Kirby asked what it was, she told him, "That's Schubert, mostly. Or Dvořák. Do you like it?"

"I never listened to classical music before, but I do like it. Very much."

She began bringing some of her own CDs from home.

The library was well stocked with reference books. After a day or two of resisting the impulse to make notes in the margins Kirby went to the nearest drugstore and bought a spiral notebook and a box of lead pencils. He discovered the advantage of bibliographies and started tracking concepts from one source to another.

He began to recognize patterns. He began to have ideas of his own.

Whole days went by during which Kirby did not think about his face at all.

Leon Sparks was apologetic. "I'm sorry, Mrs. Delmonico, but I don't have any news for you. It's been over three months and there's no sign of Kirby."

"At least you haven't found his . . . his . . ."

"Body. No ma'am, and between us I don't think we will. America's a big country; if someone doesn't want to be found it's almost impossible to find them. We'll keep him on the missing persons list a while longer, but don't get your hopes up. He'll . . ."

"I know, he'll come home when he's ready."

"I believe he will," Bea told Gloria. "I think we should make arrangements for the plastic surgeon now, so when Kirby does show up things will be ready for him. We can't wait for Tilbury Memorial; we'll take Kirby to whatever hospital his surgeon has operating privileges in."

"But there will be a Tilbury Memorial Hospital, won't there?"

"Oh yes," said Bea. "Yes indeed. Jack is taking care of the financial details right now."

Bea made Jack's role sound simpler than it was. In the chaotic aftermath of the war crime was flourishing. While the country was under attack some citizens who were law-abiding under ordinary circumstances had discovered opportunities to make a little money on the side. A cautious fling on the black market; a clever theft.

Networks already on the shady side of the law had also expanded. When the shooting stopped they did not declare a truce on their new enterprises.

Jack knew he would have no trouble unloading the gold, though he could not walk into the central bank and ask for cash. "I'll be selling the gold a bit at a time, Aunt Bea; we don't want anyone to guess that you have a hoard here."

"The money has to go toward Kirby's surgery first."

"I understand that. No matter how expensive it is, it'll be cheaper than rebuilding a hospital. Have you decided on a plastic surgeon yet?"

"They all insist they have to see Kirby first, but there is a man in Madison who sounded really interested; he's worked on similar cases before. I didn't tell him Kirby was missing, only that he isn't available right now. I promised we'd make an appointment soon."

"You don't usually make promises you can't keep, Aunt Bea."

"I'm hoping, Jack; Gloria and I are both hoping, that's all we can do."

Converting gold bars to cash without involving the federal government meant transporting them beyond the state capital; Jack's network of connections was far flung. Traveling for any considerable distance by horse-bus or pony-and-trap was impracticable, but since metal alloys had ceased to disintegrate automobiles were appearing on the road again. Sycamore River now boasted a car-rental business. It had just opened, and the cars were exorbitantly overpriced, since it had no competition so far.

"Would you be willing to go with me?" Jack asked Gerry. "I need somebody to ride shotgun."

"You expecting to get robbed on the way?"

"No, but I'm always expecting trouble."

"Is a real shotgun involved?"

"My Walther P38. Can you handle it?"

"I don't know if I could actually shoot anybody."

"Here's a fact I've observed, Gerry. A man's ability to fight is in direct proportion to his ability to love. Now, do you want to go with me or not?"

"Count on it."

The car Jack rented was so new it still smelled like embalming fluid. He had asked rather wistfully for a red convertible; he had been given a black sedan.

"I want a manual, not an autonomous," he had specified to the rental agent. "I prefer to do the driving myself."

"You'll like this model," the man assured him, "the air-conditioning's top class, it'll freeze your balls. There's no spare tire in the trunk, but I'll have a spare for you next week, Mr. Reece."

"Don't bother; I want the trunk empty."

Jack was unhappy about being away while Nell was ill. Her breathing was increasingly ragged. At his insistence a doctor had come out from Sycamore River to examine Nell. He brought antibiotics and an oxygen tank with him. He told Jack, "Your wife really should be in a hospital. She needs more than you can provide here."

"You don't happen to have a spare hospital in your medical bag, do you? The nearest thing we have is maternity only, and Nell's a little too sick to get her pregnant right now."

The doctor did not know if Jack was joking. He said, "We lost far too many hospitals in the war. I personally think the bastards targeted them on purpose."

Nell fought back a cough to ask, "Did we target theirs?"

He did not answer.

Nell hated the oxygen tank, hated having to put the mask over her nose and mouth. "It doesn't do any good, Jack; the oxygen just makes the burning worse. I think that man's a quack."

"Gloria knows him, she says he has a fine reputation."

"Gloria thinks well of everybody."

Jack lay awake at night, listening to his wife's breathing. Occasionally it stopped, making the skin prickle on his scalp. Before he could act the labored breathing resumed.

"Nell?"

"Wha-?"

"You're not breathing."

"Of course I am; did you wake me up to tell me that?"

Every aspect of Jack's life had become stressful. Nell had been his refuge; now she was his greatest worry.

He was not a man to confide in others, but late one evening when he was tired and his defenses were low, he told Lila Ragland, "When I was a boy I had a pal who didn't want a dog because it would hurt too much when it died. Now I understand."

She said, "I hope you told your pal the answer was to get another dog."

Thinking about her words afterward, Jack knew it was good advice: like getting back on a horse after you fall off. He needed a dose of good advice.

On the morning of his trip with Gerry he came awake before the alarm went off, reluctantly swimming upward through layers of semiconsciousness.

Aware of Nell's body so close to his own.

An hour later he and Gerry, with gold bars wrapped in newspaper under the floor of the car's trunk, headed west. Their route took them through the agricultural heartland of the state. The two men were taken aback by what they saw. Some farms had been abandoned outright. Others were just barely hanging on, waging a doomed battle against crop failure in the unrelenting drought. It was hard to imagine that this area had once been the pride of the state, a fertile testimony to hard work and skillful husbandry. An idyllic place to raise a family.

There was no evidence of nuclear attack here, but a rural

village at a crossroad had been struck by conventional bombs that destroyed the general store and a schoolhouse and left a crater in the road.

Jack carefully maneuvered around the crater and drove on. After half a mile they saw a cornfield—or what had been a cornfield—beside the road. The stalks still stood upright, though they were parched and brown. The corn had not been harvested but left to rot. Relentless heat had split the shocks apart to reveal a few stunted grains clinging to gray corncobs.

Jack stopped the car. Folding his arms on top of the steering wheel, he gazed bleakly at the ruined crop. "Tell me, Gerry; how can we win the war?"

"I thought we did."

"I wasn't talking about fighting the eastern bloc, I was talking about the war against our climate. Dammit, I wish Edgar was still here. He might have some ideas; that old grouch was the sanest man in this whole crazy world."

"We miss people the most after they're dead."

Jack turned to look at Gerry. "Maybe we do; there's a lesson in there." He started the car and drove on, deliberately keeping his eyes on the road rather than seeing the landscape.

Their destination was a seedy motel beyond Crystal Lake. Six shabby white cottages off the main road, absolutely identical, with every trace of individuality expunged. Jack parked in front of one of the cottages. A large mongrel chained to a post thundered a challenge, but Jack ignored it. "Wait here," he told Gerry. "I'd introduce you but you wouldn't like this guy."

He rapped on the front door with his knuckles. One-two, one-three. The door opened slightly and a conversation took place. Jack nodded and stepped back. A fat man wearing baggy khaki shorts and a sweat-stained undershirt came outside and followed Jack to the car. He raised the lid of the trunk.

From where he was sitting Gerry could not see what happened next, but after several minutes he heard the fat man grunt. He stood up holding an oblong package wrapped in newspapers while Jack slammed the lid of the trunk. The fat man carried his burden into the cottage; Jack got in the car and drove away.

"I said you wouldn't like him," he remarked to Gerry as he turned back onto the main road.

"But who the hell is he?"

"Mister Fifty Thousand Dollars. Fortunately there are more men like him; we'll be visiting them too."

"How the hell do you know people like that?"

Jack laughed.

"When Kirby comes home he can have his surgery, Aunt Bea." Jack handed her a thick, legal-sized manila folder. "Keep this money safe. You'll find it's more than enough."

"How about hiding it in one of Edgar's tunnels?"

Jack smiled. "Couldn't be better."

Satisfied with the day's work, he went to be with Nell.

There was a smear of fresh blood on her pillow.

Jack felt suddenly and unbearably weary. He had relied on his strength for so long—he and everyone else—that feeling it desert him was a shock. His legs were rubbery. He abruptly sat down on the bed beside her, sliding one hand over the pillow to hide the blood.

Maybe she hadn't seen it.

Maybe he could simply make it go away.

When he bent to kiss her, the willing lips she raised to meet his were dry and cracked. Dry and cracked like the corn; everything burned up and dying. . . . He passed his hand over his eyes. "Sorry sweetheart, I'm just . . ."

"Exhausted? You look it. Go have a nice cool shower, then Bea will give you supper."

"Have you already eaten?"

She gave a tiny shrug. "I'm not very hungry."

"I won't eat unless you do."

"Blackmail?" Nell smiled up at him. "Lila's always said you look like a pirate."

"When did you and Lila discuss me?"

"What do you think we do all day? It's like being in the shelter; we talk about everything."

"I'm not sure I like your discussing me behind my back."

"Don't be touchy, Jack. Lila's very fond of you, she would do anything for you."

He arched an eyebrow. "Good to know."

19

Shay Mulligan had never asked Lila to marry him. To Shay, love was quantifiable. He was fond of Lila but not in the way he had loved Evan's mother. When she died the ability to feel intense emotion had dried up in him. He had never explained this to Lila and she had never asked. They were good friends who gave each other physical comfort. The arrangement seemed to suit them both.

After the episode with Kirby brought Evan's relationship with Jess to light, Shay felt he had to question his son. "Do you want to marry Jess?"

"Someday," Evan said evasively.

"Sexual mores may have changed drastically but a few truths remain, including what my grandfather said to me. He warned me not to sleep with a girl unless I was willing to marry her."

"I am willing to marry Jess, Dad; I want to take her with me to Mars Settlement when it's ready. As a married couple we'd get priority. I have all the information already."

"You're determined to do that? I thought Mars was a dream you'd get over."

"Look what we've done to this planet! We've ruined it; nobody in their right minds would want to have children here. It's time to start over fresh."

"What makes you think we won't do the same thing again on Mars?"

Evan was horrified. "Don't you think we've learned our lesson?"

"I don't think so at all." Shay Mulligan looked at the hopeful face of his only son and wished he could give him a better answer. "The last thing the human race really *learned* was to walk upright."

Shay had a lot on his mind. He was worried about what would happen if . . . or when . . . Kirby came home again. There was bound to be a confrontation; perhaps violent. How reassuring it would be if Evan was on Mars by then, though that could take years.

On the other hand, Shay hated the idea of his son being so far away.

He tried to imagine what it would be like to live on Mars. A frontier life on a very different frontier. He had seen the photographs, everyone had seen the photographs; almost like a Hollywood movie set except the distant heavenly body in the sky wasn't a film star, it was Earth. Evan was enthusiastic about the prospect; young people accepted the idea of going to Mars Settlement just as their ancestors had accepted migrating from the Old World to the New.

Distance isn't the great divider, Shay thought to himself. Time is. Time is the abyss.

Time and death.

Nell thought about dying. She should not think about it but hold only positive thoughts, yet somewhere in her mind there was a door. If that door swung open there would be dark on the other side. Oblivion. And sooner or later she was going to have to step through.

Everyone does.

Once she woke up in the middle of the night shouting "No!"

Jack was frightened; he rightly guessed what she had been dreaming but she denied it. "It was only a nightmare about falling down stairs."

"Tomorrow I'm going to take you to the state capital. There are several hospitals still open and you're going into one. Gloria's given me the name of a thoracic specialist who . . ."

"No, darling, please! You don't know how bad my chest hurts, I can't bear the thought of a long drive."

"Not long, it'll take less than an hour, and then we'll have you in a hospital bed and . . ."

She fought for breath. "You're not listening to me, Jack; I don't want to go anywhere." The pain in her throat and chest was like talons clawing her flesh, ripping their way from the inside out. Every day was worse than the one before, just as every day was hotter.

The door in her mind was clearly visible now. Slowly opening.

In the morning Lila stayed with Nell while Jack went for the rental car. He opened all the car doors and windows and switched on the fan to help the pent-up heat escape, then drove home with the air-conditioning turned up to the max. After Lila helped him spread sheets and arrange pillows on the back seat, he asked, "Would you mind going with us? I'll drive as carefully as I can but I need you to help steady her."

He carried Nell out to the car, protesting all the way. Being carried from the house to the car set off a spasm of coughing. Lila sat on the back seat with her. She did not envy Nell now; the other woman's suffering was painful to witness.

When they reached the hospital two white-uniformed attendants came out with a gurney. Their crisp professionalism was reassuring. "She'll be all right now, Mr. Reece, we'll take good care of her. Doctor Peters will examine her in a few minutes and then he'll probably want her taken straight to a bed. If you and your friend would like to sit in the waiting room, a nurse will come for you when your wife's ready to see you."

"Slam, bam, thank you ma'am," Jack said to Lila. "They don't waste any time, do they? I should have brought Nell here sooner, whether she was willing or not."

"She was afraid of this, Jack. People who are never sick are often terrified of hospitals."

They sat together in the waiting room for over an hour, then went to the cafeteria for a lunch that neither wanted. Trying to make small talk to distract him, Lila said, "The summit starts tomorrow in Philadelphia. The commentator on the radio said they're going to discuss denuclearization."

"That's been discussed over and over again," Jack replied, "but neither side's willing to give up their nuclear weapons. Every politician and militarist insists they need them for their own protection."

"Well, they do—as long as someone else has nukes too. Nobody wants to allow their adversaries an advantage; it's a real *Catch-22* situation."

Jack was pleasantly surprised by the reference. "Do you like twentieth-century novels?" he asked. *"Portnoy's Complaint,* for example?"

"I think it's hilarious, but I prefer more serious work from that era. Have you read anything by Norman Mailer? And what about our contemporary writers like Jesse Scrivener and Mary Macy?"

They were still discussing books when a nurse arrived to take Jack to Nell's private room. He found her propped against pillows, with a faint flush of color in her cheeks. "They've given me some medication for the pain," she told him, "and put me on a drip for hydration. I'm feeling better already. I didn't have to go through the door after all."

"What door?"

"Oh, nothing"—she made a deprecating gesture—"just me being foolish. My problem isn't even that unusual; my doctor's dealing with two other cases of it. He thinks it's a reaction to something in the atmosphere."

"Wait until I tell Gerry. He suspects the ratio of atmospheric gases has changed, and he may be right."

"Another change," Nell murmured to herself.

"Lila's with me, she's waiting outside. Would you like to see her?"

Lila's with me. At those words, Nell's subconscious uttered a warning. Lila was always with Jack now. Sexy, healthy, clever Lila who had such a way with men.

Nell put a pale hand on Jack's arm. "I'm a little tired now," she temporized. "Maybe some other time."

"Okay, we should be getting home anyway. I'll see you again tomorrow; is there anything you want me to bring for you?"

We should be getting home. Now Nell knew the face of her enemy. Not the climate, but a woman she had thought was a friend.

Very well. She would fight. Eleanor Richmond Bennett Reece would show the world that she could fight.

"When you come tomorrow don't bring Lila," she said to Jack. "Jess might like to come instead and I'd rather see her. I'm always glad to see Lila too, but she has her own life to live. Hospital visits are no fun and she gets bored so easily."

"Lila does?"

"That's why she goes from man to man," Nell lied, "and

occasionally to a woman. Not me, of course!" she added with a little laugh.

There, Lila Ragland; let's see if my husband still finds you attractive!

That evening Jack told Gerry about Nell's diagnosis. "Climatologists are conducting tests worldwide," he said, "and the medical profession's beginning to sit up and take note. Doctor Peters told me the scientific findings support your theory, there's definitely been a change in the global atmosphere. It appears that some people, like Nell, are more sensitive to it than others."

"What can be done about it?"

"Overall? Nothing, except hope it doesn't get any worse. Maybe future generations will evolve to deal with it. For now there are medications and therapies to enable a person to live with the condition. It's a bit like having asthma or a serious allergy. As I told Kirby once, animals don't acknowledge handicaps, they just get on with their lives. We'll have to do that too."

"How's Nell handling it?"

"I married a Thoroughbred. She'll cope."

"That," said Gerry, "is the best compliment I ever heard a man pay to his wife."

"Speaking of Kirby—is there still no sign of him?"

"Not a whisker. I think he fell off the planet."

The pair were sitting on Veronica's balcony with a bottle of whiskey and a pitcher of water on the table between them. Jack had been drinking more than his share but he was not feeling it. When he had a lot on his mind his metabolism was resistant to alcohol. "Here's a question for a scientist, Gerry. What could have altered the atmosphere?"

"This is only speculation, but the introduction of a different gas might do it. Not the usual ones, but something else."

"Where did it come from? Could our enemies have . . ."

"Not on a planetary scale," Gerry interrupted. "It would have to be a natural phenomenon."

"Like the Change?"

"I never believed the Change was a natural phenomenon, Jack; I've always thought there was a human agency behind it. But the situation with the atmosphere is different. A geologic change might be involved, one affecting the magma deep inside the planet and causing the production of dangerous gases. Under normal conditions gases have a density a thousand times greater than liquids. Gas is highly compressible but it tends to expand indefinitely when released. Remember Kirby's discovery in that book of Edgar's? 'Matter tells space and time to curve. Space and time tell matter to move.'

"There are toxic gases inside this planet that don't reach the surface under normal conditions, but a volcanic eruption may release them. There have been a lot of volcanic eruptions in recent years. Or suppose an even more powerful force expressed all of them at once? Literally squeezed them out?"

Jack looked dubious. "That's what's wrong with theories; they aren't facts. There's no force on earth capable of doing what you suggest."

20

On the following morning Bea decided to hide what she thought of as "Kirby's money" in the most remote of the tunnels. She did not like going down into the shelter alone, but reminded herself that it had been home and sanctuary for many weeks. Were it not for Edgar's bolt-hole they might all be dead.

Her most comfortable walking shoes were at the back of the closet; the biggest flashlight was on a top shelf in the kitchen. As she climbed the hill toward the barn Samson trotted behind her, panting. The sun beat down on upon them both. Its heat was reflected back to them from the hard-baked earth. Before she had gone halfway Bea was soaked with perspiration.

She hoped Buster would be in the barn with the Silkies, so she could ask him to accompany her to the tunnels. But though he had put fresh water in the chickens' water pans, he was gone. She patted the horses and stroked their velvet noses before she opened the door to the shelter. When she flicked on the light switch just inside, her confidence returned.

"You wait for me up here," she told Samson. "You're too heavy for me to carry." The big Rottweiler sat down obediently. Halfway down the stairs Bea was met by cooler air; welcoming air.

Memories flooded over her. Being in the shelter had been like living in another world. She and Edgar had discovered their feelings for each other in this place. Although war was going on outside, they had been happy.

If only we could go back, she thought.

She was careful of her footing in the tunnels. If she fell and hurt herself, no one would know where she was. When she reached her destination and tucked the envelope behind a stack of boxes she was relieved. As she turned around, she thought she heard something skittering behind her. Bea stopped; stood very still, listening. No sound.

I must be imagining things.

The heat enveloped her again as she reached the top of the stairs. Its intensity made her dizzy. Eager to return to the air-conditioned house, she left the barn and hurried down the hill with Samson at her heels. She did not watch her footing but tripped and fell, hard, knocking the breath out of her lungs.

Bea lay on the side of the hill, scolding herself. Silly old woman, she thought, you should have been more careful.

Samson began licking her face. Her skirt had ridden up, giving her a glimpse of the swollen veins in her legs.

I am a silly *old* woman.

The admission was worse than the fall. While Edgar lived and loved her she was young inside; they were both young inside. Today on this sun-scorched hillside she felt the last of her youth burned away.

When Bea pushed the dog aside and tried to get up, her

traitor body deserted her. She rolled onto her side, intending to get to her hands and knees, but lacked the strength. After a futile struggle she lay back down again to rest before a second attempt. Samson closed in to cover her face with sloppy kisses.

It was not as bad as if she had fallen in the tunnels; at least here she would be visible from the house. Then she remembered that Jack had gone to visit Nell in the hospital. If she was still lying here when he returned, Bea would be embarrassed.

She had to get up.

Another try, levering herself with arms that refused to obey her.

The glaring sun was like a broiler, cooking her.

She looked longingly toward the house, which seemed so far away now. In the bright light she could make out the belt of evergreen shrubbery that encircled the foundation.

With a superhuman effort Bea began to drag herself down the hill toward the touch of green.

Jack was depressed when he returned from the hospital. Jess had intended going with him but she was catching a cold and did not want to give it to her mother. Nell did not appear to be making any progress, though the doctor assured him she was. "It's just a little bit at a time, we're waiting for sensitive tissues to heal and it won't happen overnight."

Jack went to visit Nell every day. He bought the black sedan from the car rental agency for convenience.

There was a time when Jack was what his Aunt Bea described as "finicky" about cars; a scarlet Mustang convertible had been his pride and joy. After the Mustang fell victim to the Change, Jack's passion for cars had dwindled. He bought the sedan simply because it was there.

"Men have been known to marry unsuitable women for the same reason," Shay Mulligan remarked.

On the way to the hospital Jack drove too fast; going home was a different story. Without Nell in the house he was in no hurry. From the front lane he could not see the hillside. He parked the car in the shade of the house and went in.

"Anybody home?"

The Irish setters came running to greet him. Shay's black cat followed them at a leisurely pace; Karma was beginning to feel the first twinges of age and would not hurry for anyone.

"Anybody home?" Jack called again. "Jess, Aunt Bea, are you here?"

Aside from the panting of the setters the house was quiet, but Jack could hear the deep bark of the Rottweiler somewhere outside.

Jack went into the kitchen to get a glass of water. As he stood at the sink he glanced out the window above it . . . and saw Bea lying on the hillside. Samson was pawing at her in anxiety.

Jack dropped the glass; it shattered on the floor as he ran outside.

"Aunt Bea! My god, Aunt Bea! What happened?"

She regained consciousness in his arms. With Samson following close behind, Jack carried her into the house. Bea was confused; she reached up and touched his face with feverish fingertips. "My baby," she said hoarsely. "My son Jack. You have your father's eyes."

Within a few minutes the others appeared for lunch. Jess burst into tears when Jack told her about Bea's accident. Gloria diagnosed her condition as heat stroke. So did the doctor, who did not like to make house calls; he came out to the farm for a second time because Jack Reece intimidated him. "You've done the right thing by packing your aunt in ice," the man said. "Untreated she could have had brain damage." He left medication for Bea with explicit instructions on its use. "I don't suppose I need to ask you to call me if there's any change in her condition?" he remarked to Jack.

"You know I will." A muscle twitched in Jack's jaw. "And I'll expect you to drop everything and get the hell out here. Or send an ambulance."

The afternoon was very quiet. Even the twins tiptoed.

With the crisis over, Jack had time to think. *My baby. My son Jack.*

When he was a little boy he had accepted without question what Bea told him. "Your father and your mother were killed in a car crash. As your nearest relative I was allowed to adopt you but I didn't change your surname to mine. I thought you'd want to keep your father's name."

As he grew older Jack had begun to puzzle over his origin. Bea Fontaine had a massive photo album crammed with pictures of family and friends dating back to her own grandparents. On rainy days he liked to sit down with it and ask his Aunt Bea to identify the faces and tell the stories that went with them. All he had of his history were his aunt, the house he grew up in, and those faces.

The one that belonged to Cameron Reece had Jack's strong cheekbones and hawkish nose, but he could see nothing of himself in the picture of Florence Reece.

In the college photographs of Beatrice Fontaine he recognized his own mouth and chin.

Children like to imagine they come from dramatic backgrounds, such as being kidnapped from a royal family. Bit by bit Jack had pieced together a truth for himself that was not quite the story Bea told him. By the time he was a grown man he was his own construction, a complex personality embodying the qualities he chose in addition to those dictated by his genes. This gave him an indefinable mystery that men and women alike found attractive.

No one really knew Jack Reece, though Nell came the closest. He decided to get the true story while Bea was still alive to tell him. If she had kept it a secret for so long she must have her reasons.

Strategy was one of Jack's strong points. He always took advantage of an opportunity.

She appeared to be asleep when he went into her room, but

as soon as he sat down in the armchair beside the bed she opened her eyes. "Jack?"

"The one and only," he said. "Your baby, your son Jack. Who has his father's eyes."

Bea stiffened on the bed. She had been expecting this moment for so long; dreading it, rehearsing what she would say. Her mouth went dry. "Can we . . . talk about this later?"

That meant she needed time to prepare and he didn't want to give her time; he wanted the truth before she could erect shields. "You gave yourself away a while ago," he said.

She closed her eyes again. "I don't know what you're talking about."

"Yes, you do. Was I an illegitimate baby?"

"There's no such thing as an illegitimate baby, Jack; every baby who's born is a genuine baby."

"You're playing with words," he accused. "Florence Reece wasn't my birth mother, was she." Not a question; a statement.

"No, she wasn't."

"Why didn't you tell me? I have a right to know who I am."

"And you do know; you're John Cameron Reece, the same man you were five minutes ago. Is this so important? Look at the Nyeberger boys; they're the Delmonico boys now and it doesn't seem to trouble them at all."

"Kirby is very troubled."

"That has nothing to do with his being adopted. Please, Jack, let this go; it hurts me. I don't have much emotional resilience anymore."

"I don't want to hurt you, Aunt . . . Bea. Look, I don't even know what to call you."

She propped herself on one elbow so she could see his face. "Aunt Bea will do. It's been just fine for years."

She kept watching his face while she related the story; the unfortunate love affair with a university lecturer, the marriage of her sister to the man Bea had still loved. Her decision to give them her infant son so he would have two parents.

When she finished, Jack was quiet for a measureless time while she waited with a pounding heart. Then he gave Bea the brilliant Jack Reece smile. "I'm proud to have you for a mother."

He told Nell about it two days later, choosing a time when Jess did not accompany him to the hospital.

"Your Aunt Bea's certainly full of surprises," Nell commented when Jack had finished. "She makes me wonder how many other people have skeletons in their closets, things they don't share even with their nearest and dearest. I never talk about Robert Bennett and the life I lived with him; I'd rather pull out my fingernails with pliers."

She had told Jack the intimate details of her marriage to a misogynistic bully, but only after she felt sure of his love. He had listened without comment and never mentioned the subject again.

Now he said, "We're talking about a little thing called the human condition, Nell. Most of us are carrying a lot of baggage by the end of our lives; it can be an awful burden if we let it. But remember Edgar's remark: Death is the get-out-of-jail card."

21

As always, Lila had been monitoring the news. Although she was no longer working as a reporter for *The Sycamore Seed* she devoured current events the way another woman might devour soap operas. When the electricity was restored she had promptly bought a radio for the room she shared with Shay, a reproduction with a twentieth-century plastic body. The cessation of the Change had brought fake antiquities into fashion.

If Lila was in the room the radio was always on.

Even when they were in bed together.

Shay was used to it, the way a waiter got used to background music in a restaurant. If he came in and the radio was off he turned it on automatically.

On the first evening when Bea felt like coming to the table, they were just sitting down to supper when Lila burst into the room, alight with excitement. "It's official! I just heard the announcement from Philadelphia!"

Gerry put down his fork. "They rang the Liberty Bell again and this time it didn't crack?"

"Better than that. The government has signed a binding declaration of peace with the alliance of our enemies. Denuclearization is beginning at once. *On both sides.* The war is really over!"

They had to wait for the words to sink in; it was too much to absorb all at once. A battered planet that had endured one world war after another was finally going to have peace.

"It sounds too good to be true," Gloria murmured. She could feel herself choking up.

"It's true all right. On the radio I could hear horns honking and sirens shrieking and people shouting for joy in Philadelphia. If Times Square hadn't been destroyed it would be jammed with the largest party ever."

"There's nothing to stop us having our own victory party," said Jack. "There must be a bottle of champagne around here somewhere. Edgar wouldn't have overlooked the possibility of peace breaking out."

Bea replied, "That's the one possibility he did overlook. You knew Edgar, he was so sure mankind was going to destroy itself."

"I'm damned glad he was wrong. C'mon, let's see what we have to celebrate with."

A diligent search of the house failed to discover any champagne, or even any remaining Jameson whiskey, but nothing could dampen the high spirits at Tilbury Farm. "There's going to be a helluva lot of rebuilding and replacing needed," Gerry predicted. "This country's going to see a fantastic boom in construction; if Edgar was still around he'd be right in the thick of it. There'll be jobs for everyone. What do you think, Evan? Would you like to be an apprentice carpenter?"

"No thanks; I'd rather be an apprentice Martian."

Gerry laughed. "You're not serious."

"Yes, I am."

"He is," Shay concurred, "but I'm trying to talk him out of it."

The party lasted until dawn, when accompanied by their dogs and some of their cats, they trooped out onto the lawn to greet the rising sun.

Gerry noticed the luxuriant green of the foundation plantings around the house. "Hey, Muffin," he called to Gloria, "come see these bushes. Everything else is dead, but they're alive and thriving. How do you account for that?"

"Several days ago I gave them a couple of buckets of water."

"Was that enough to keep them this green?"

Gloria shook her head. "I wouldn't have thought so. I meant to keep watering them but with so much going on it slipped my mind."

Shay and Evan were walking together, discussing Mars Settlement. Shay was urging his son to consider a vet practice on Earth, "So I can visit you," but the glamour of Mars outweighed his arguments. "Rocket ships travel both ways, Dad; once I'm out there, you can visit me. Take a few months off."

How could a mere father compete with another world?

Bea leaned heavily on Jack's arm but she had refused to be

left behind. "I wish Nell were here to share this moment," she said.

"So do I," Jess agreed. "I hope they've been told about it in the hospital."

"I imagine they have," said Jack. "The patients are probably banging their bedpans together right now; there's no tonic like good news." He turned to the woman leaning on his arm. "If you can stand more good news, Nell's doctor expects to send her home in a few more days."

"It isn't too soon, is it?"

"I don't think so, he's a man who errs on the side of caution."

"You're the exact opposite," Bea replied. "I'm surprised the two of you get along."

"I can get along with anyone," Jack said blandly. "Anyone who agrees with me."

A chill wind was rising; a salmon-colored flush filled the eastern sky. The light was reflected in their faces.

Jess gave a sudden gasp. "Who's that coming toward us? Is it . . . it *is*, it's Kirby!" She ran toward him.

When Evan saw Jess running he started after her—as she flung herself into Kirby's arms. He dropped the suitcase he was carrying to hold her instead.

"You're back! I'm so glad! Where have you been, why'd you go away, why didn't you at least phone, we were so worried, why . . ."

"Take it easy," Kirby laughed, "you're strangling me."

Flustered, she released him and took a couple of steps back-ward. The warm imprint of her body clung to him.

"I thought you were mad at me," Kirby said as he stooped to pick up his suitcase.

"I wasn't, not at all, but Evan and I . . . well, we thought you were mad at us."

"No."

"Then it was just a misunderstanding?"

"I don't think you could call it that, Jess; I understood what I saw. But if you and Evan . . ."

By now Evan was standing behind Jess, looking over her shoulder at Kirby.

"We're not," Jess said. "I mean . . . it's just casual with us, it's not like we're in love or anything."

Evan felt an almost overwhelming desire to punch Kirby in the face; his mutilated face. But he couldn't do that to a man who was so disfigured. Instead he locked eyes with Kirby—or tried to; one eye was elusive—and let the other man see the extent of his loathing.

The trio were frozen in the moment.

Jess broke the spell. "Where have you been, Kirby?" she asked again. "You were gone for months! Poor Gloria filed a missing persons complaint and the police printed posters. We were afraid you might be dead." Her voice caught in her throat.

"I needed to look for something."

"What could be so important that . . ."

"Myself. I had to find myself."

"What pretentious bullshit!" said Evan.

Jess ignored him. "And did you find Kirby Delmonico?" she asked softly.

Kirby nodded. Smiled with the intact side of his lips.

She smiled back.

A silent conversation was going on between the two of them, Evan thought. By not speaking aloud they were locking him out.

The two young men had grown up in the same town, gone to the same schools, played on the same teams. They had been friends for years—until it changed in the blink of an eye and something irreplaceable was lost.

Kirby's homecoming vied with the declaration of peace as a cause for celebration. Happiness on a personal scale and joy on a global scale.

The unanswered questions about the period when Kirby was missing were temporarily set aside by tacit agreement; his temper was well known, why allow it to spoil the occasion? Gloria said, "He'll tell us when he's ready."

Kirby chose to make an occasion of it. As he had done once before, he came to the dinner table carrying a book: a large spiral notebook this time. He set it down in front of Jack.

Evan suspected Kirby was planning to steal his thunder by writing a journal of his own. The sneaky son of a bitch.

Jack read the first page to himself. Then aloud. "The dictionary defines 'sentience' as being capable of thinking and feeling, by which is meant thinking and feeling like a human. Can we know how other life forms think and feel? The thoughts of a whale may be as far beyond our ken as our thoughts are beyond those of termites. Or maybe the thoughts of termites are superior to ours and we are unaware of it because we can't communicate with them."

Jack looked up at Kirby. "Where did this come from?"

"From me. Remember the quote from Einstein's speech? You were impressed because I'd connected that particular quote with the Change. When you were impressed I started to have a little faith in myself. While I was away I began to test my limits, or it might be more accurate to say 'push the envelope.' I found a public library better stocked than Edgar's and a patient librarian who let me spend all day, every day there.

"That's when I started writing down my thoughts, like the one about sentience. As I explored what was going on in my own head I began to reach out for more. More facts, more understanding; I could almost feel myself growing. I realized my face isn't *me*."

"I could have told you that," said Jess.

Evan was struggling to control his temper. This "prodigal son" routine of Kirby's wasn't fooling him. "You're full of crap, Kirby. Let me see that notebook of yours." Evan reached out and grabbed it.

Kirby made no effort to stop him.

Evan turned to another page. Expecting to pour scorn on Kirby's words, he began to read aloud. "Is it possible that other entities possessed of awareness and volition can develop parallel to cellular life? Life as we understand it is carbon based, but suppose stones, which are also carbon based, have an evolved sentience unlike our own, yet just as real. Could this be what underlies the theory of a universal mind?"

Evan looked up from the page. They were all watching him intently.

"Go on," Jack urged.

Evan resumed reading. "In our solar system the building blocks of life are carbon and the energy of the sun, but that does not mean the rest of the universe follows the same pattern. In fact it is extremely unlikely; the universe is immense and offers immense opportunity for variation. There might be gaseous life-forms out there somewhere and others that are pure spirit. For all we know, planets themselves might be life-forms. The Earth beneath our feet may be able to act in its own self interest."

Gloria caught her breath. "Perhaps the planet has recognized humans as dangerous parasites! Maybe that's why we've been having the heat and the terrible storms: to rid the world of us."

Shay shook his head. "That's ordinary nature at work. If there's any truth to this hypothesis the planet hasn't been attacking us directly, it's been destroying the man-made objects that are dangerous to itself."

"Wait a minute here," said Lila. "Are you implying *Earth* is sentient?"

Jack felt goose bumps rise along his arms.

22

"Mother Earth," Gloria breathed.

"That's a myth," said Gerry. "An ancient fertility symbol."

"Myth?" Jack cocked an eyebrow. "Every myth contains a seed of truth. Two hundred years ago a self-trained German archaeologist named Heinrich Schliemann refused to believe the poetry of Homer was based on myth. So he went out and dug up Troy.

"Kirby, if there's any truth in your conjecture—and there well may be—then perhaps you've identified the entity behind the Change. You suggested an answer to *How*; now you may have discovered *Who*. All the pieces fit, if we just move back far enough to have a wide view."

"I've been trying to take that wide view," said Kirby. "We know that stars and planets have their own life cycles. Earth contains all of the elements needed to construct a different kind of thinking machine, not a separate brain but an integral, fully functioning part of the whole. There's no reason why the power of the planet's magnetic field couldn't be used to melt plastic or deconstruct a metal alloy.

"On Earth there's been a corresponding evolution of biota

and environment. Let's suppose the biota of the planet are its senses. A kind of radar, like a cat's whiskers, they react to their immediate environment. From the environment plants and animals collect the necessary information to optimize conditions for planetary survival. If the environment is unfavorable the planet can correct the situation. For the most part these corrections have taken place in geologic time, but recently mankind has worked a little too fast.

"In the twentieth century human beings developed a sure-fire way to destroy the world. That wasn't our intention, but it was bound to be the outcome. We couldn't save ourselves from our own ambition and greed. We needed a hero and we didn't have one.

"But by decomposing the materials man was using to cause the most damage to the planet, Earth may have saved us all."

Every eye was on Kirby; every eye but Evan's. He was astonished that the other man was so intelligent, so *clever*. He knew he was being petty but he could not help it. Kirby's scars did not repulse Jess; apparently his mind made up for his face.

Jess was looking at him as if he were a film star.

But she's gone to bed with me, damn it! I'm sure she's never gone to . . . would never go to . . .

Evan had a horrifying mental picture of the girl he loved in bed with an ogre.

———

After dinner he waited for Jess to leave the dining room. Most of them were still in there, gathered around Kirby. Evan gritted his teeth.

Come on, will you? Come on!

When she came through the doorway Evan caught her by her arm. "I need to talk to you, Jess, right away. It's urgent."

"Is my mom all right?"

"This isn't about her, it's about you. You and me. Come on, let's go out on the porch."

She was puzzled but she followed him. Jess never liked to make a scene.

When they were sitting side by side on the porch steps, Evan resisted the temptation to put his arm around her. She must not feel pressured. "You told me you don't want to commit to marriage right now," he began, "and I respect that. But I've decided to emigrate to Mars Settlement. Emigration won't begin for several years, so I have time to make all the arrangements. I'm not ever going to feel about anybody else the way I feel about you, Jess . . . so please tell me you'll at least think about going with me."

To Evan's surprise she didn't say no. She didn't say yes either. Instead she gazed at the darkening sky as if waiting for the first star to appear. "Colonists have to take a really stringent medical exam," Jess said, without looking at him. "I've even heard they have to be tattooed."

"Well, yes," he replied reluctantly. "Your identity code, your blood type and RH factor, plus your immunities and inoculations. But it's okay, for women they do it with an invisible ink that only shows up under infrared light."

"That is a comfort." He couldn't tell if Jess was being sarcastic or not. "Why are you so anxious to go, Evan? The war's over and things are going to get back to normal. Why run away from home?"

"I'm not running away from, I'm running to. Mars is something I've always wanted."

"Well, don't let me keep you," she said huffily. Seeing the disappointment on his face she relented. "My mom's seriously ill, Evan, and I don't want to leave her. I'm not going to Mars or anywhere else with you, not right now."

Not right now.

His heart soared.

Evan was an honest young man; he would not lie to his father by saying Jess had agreed to marry him, but he could shade the truth. He told Shay, "Jess and I have been talking about getting married so we can emigrate to Mars Settlement."

Shay tried not to show the shock he felt. "And Jess is willing to do that? You surprise me. Have you talked to Nell and Jack? I wonder how they feel about having her go so far away."

"We haven't talked to them yet," Evan admitted. "You're the first person I've told."

Shay narrowed his eyes. "I know that look. You're about to ask me for money, right? Enough money to send you millions of miles from Sycamore River?"

"Well, er . . ."

"They're advertising for colonists years ahead of time, aren't they? It sounds like the government's finally got smart. How much of the project's going to come out of Uncle Sam's pockets, and how much will the colonists be paying for?"

"I couldn't tell you exactly," Evan said. "To begin with we have to send in application money with our forms."

Shay folded his arms.

"I want to send mine as early as possible," Evan continued eagerly, "so I can go with the first band of settlers. Before the flight we also have to pay for a round-trip ticket to Mars, but if we stay there for five years we get a refund for the unused portion of the ticket."

Shay said, "I suppose the agency keeps the interest on that money? What are the financial arrangements going to be like out there? I'm sure you can't telephone home for money whenever you need it. Will there be banks on Mars?"

Evan bit his lip. "I didn't ask about that, but I guess we'll have to have a bank. Colonists won't be allowed to take any stateside money with them, we'll use Marscredits instead. We're supposed to buy an adequate supply from the agency before we leave Earth."

"What's an 'adequate' supply?" Shay challenged. "Twenty thousand dollars' worth? Half a million? And what will the rate of exchange be?"

"I'll need enough to live on for a while," Evan said vaguely. "We buy our housing from the space agency before we go.

They build that themselves; I guess they have their own contractors and all. They're going to build schools too, and stores
and a hospital; even a hydroponic plant so we can grow fruit
and vegetables. Once we get settled in we can get jobs. There's
bound to be lots of work available, especially when we start
establishing farms later on."

"So Mars Settlement's being paid for in advance with terrestrial money? That is clever. And it will be outrageously
expensive."

"I have my savings in the bank, and . . . and . . ."

Shay could see it coming. "And you thought I'd make up
the rest. I'm only a veterinarian, Evan, not an investment
banker." He unfolded his arms. "What about Jess? How's she
going to pay her way—or were you planning to do that too?"

The light had gone out of Evan's eyes.

When Shay recounted the conversation to Lila, she laughed.
"Your son is badly spoiled, Shay. I wonder what it feels like to
have a parent you can go to for money whenever you like."

"I don't have the kind of money he's looking for, Lila. Before the war I might have been able to sell half my practice and
give him that—I'd always meant for him to have it anyway—
but a veterinarian can barely make a living these days. I could
apply for a second mortgage on my house but . . ."

"That's what I mean; you spoil him. If Evan wants this so
much, let him find a way himself."

Shay had been fascinated by Lila's slanted green eyes ever
since they met. He told her they were like emeralds; not a very

original observation, but true. When he looked into them now he saw green ice.

He did not mention Mars to Lila again. If her response had been more sympathetic he might have reacted differently. As it was, he went to see Bea Tilbury and laid out the problem in front of her. She heard him through to the end with an increasingly sympathetic expression on her face.

"I'm sorry about this," Shay apologized; his ears were red with embarrassment. "I've never asked anyone for money except the loan department at the bank. In fact, you gave me my mortgage."

"You know I'm not with the bank anymore, Shay. You also know I have money. Edgar said one should never admit to having money because, as he put it, the freeloaders would come out of the woodwork."

"I'm not a freeloader and I'm not asking for myself. I'm asking for Evan, and to be honest I seriously doubt if he'll ever be able to pay it back. But it's his dream, Bea. Mars. Can you imagine having a dream as big as Mars?"

"A dream as big as Mars," Bea echoed. Her thoughts were far away for a moment but she snatched them back. "Why yes, Shay, I understand how important it is to have big dreams."

That night she set the bulging manila folder on her bed and pulled out its contents. Bundles of dollar bills in large denominations, tightly tied with string, each bearing a label. EDGAR

TILBURY MEMORIAL HOSPITAL. KIRBY'S SURGERY. NEST EGG—
this one made her smile. EMERGENCY FUNDS.

The Hospital Fund was already depleted by half; rebuilding
was well underway. Kirby's Surgery was sacrosanct. But NEST
EGG and EMERGENCY were discretionary.

She counted the bills carefully, then counted them again;
compared the total with the figures Shay had given her.

She did not carry the manila folder back to the tunnels but
tucked it under her mattress. Samson slept at the foot of the
bed every night; Edgar's treasure would be well guarded.

"I don't know how we'll ever thank you," Shay said when
she gave him the money. "This is going to be repaid in full, I'll
make sure Evan understands."

"There's no rush."

"Evan was raised to appreciate there's always a rush to repay
a debt."

Shay informed his son of Bea's generosity on the same day
Jess told Evan she definitely would not go to Mars with him.
Worse than that; she would never marry him.

"But why not?" he demanded to know. "Is there someone
else?"

"This isn't about anyone else, it's about you and me. I've
given the subject a lot of thought. You're a nice man and a
good friend and I like you very much, Evan, but that's not
enough for marriage."

"I'm in love with you!"

She shook her head. "You're not listening to what I say, you only hear what you want to hear. That's part of the problem."

When a crestfallen Evan told his father about their breakup, Shay said, "Were you relying on having a wife in order to be accepted?"

"It would have helped. They probably have enough single men applying already."

"Will you go without her?"

Evan had been asking himself the same question. "I think so, Dad. It was my dream all along, not hers. If I'm accepted I'm going to give my horses to Jess." He added with a bitterness he could not disguise, "She can find someone else to teach her to ride."

"Who knows, you may meet the right girl on Mars," Shay told him.

The right girl on Mars. The phrase sounded like a prophecy.

Shay returned a portion of the money to Bea with an explanation. "Is Evan heartbroken?" she asked.

"He thinks he is, but he's young, Bea. Young hearts don't break that easily. When I was his age I thought my heart had been broken two or three times; then I met the girl who became his mother and discovered I had a whole heart to give her."

"You still love her," Bea surmised.

"I do; I always will. Death doesn't obliterate real love, Bea."

"Does Lila understand?"

"We've never talked about it but Lila's smart and observant; she knows I can go so far but no farther."

"Would you be interested in going to Mars? I suspect your son would be delighted, and the money's here if you want it."

"Me? Going to Mars?" Shay blinked. "That's very generous of you, Bea, but the idea never crossed my mind. Besides, the maximum age for colonists is fifty, and by the time the first shipload of settlers takes off I'll be well past that. I wouldn't go anyway; I've only seen a fraction of this planet so far, and I want to visit the Rocky Mountains and the Himalayas and Rome and Madrid and Lake Como and . . . you get the idea. Earth is enough for me. I'll just stay here with Lila." He paused. "Maybe I'll think about marrying her after all."

"You're not saying that to give me a happy ending, are you?"

"No, Bea, I don't believe in happy endings. There's only one ending for life. That's why you have to pack all the happiness you can into the middle of it."

23

The ceremonies around the formal ratification of the International Declaration of Peace were broadcast to a breathlessly waiting world, glowing from wallscreens, crackling from radios, blazing from headlines. The antagonists became signatories. The enemies became, if not friends, at least fellow human beings who acknowledged each others' rights.

To the amazement of cynics on all sides, denuclearization actually began.

Thousands of representatives of the military and scientific communities were appointed to oversee the process. Deconstructing would prove to be almost as time-consuming and certainly as laborious as constructing. The nearly immortal spawn of the nuclear age required more than mere disassembling. Radioactive waste must not be flushed down toilets or dumped into the already polluted seas, and no sane government was willing to accept another nation's deadly refuse.

Solving the problem would require the best minds on the planet.

For more than six thousand years the principal passion of the human species had been warfare. The back-breaking achievements of agriculture could not compete with the testosterone-fueled glories of battle. Since the first axes were fitted with stone heads men had used them on other men. One fortune after another was made through the production of weaponry. Every royal dynasty could, if it was honest, trace its beginnings to the depredations of a warlord.

During most of that time men with their greater physical strength had dominated society. Women had been relegated to the position of auxiliaries—and mothers of the next generation of warriors. Age after age, the victims of war had lived and died and been fed to the soil or the sea. Earth had accepted them all; ashes to ashes and dust to dust.

By the latter part of the twenty-first century a societal change had taken place in parts of the world. Women in the United States had demanded equality and proved they deserved it—though a few men could not accept the obvious.

Now the fever of battle was over. The immense global effort had succeeded, but momentum could not give way to inertia overnight. It took days and weeks, months even, before any changes became obvious. They appeared on a miniscule scale first: The smallest flying mammal on the planet, Kitti's hog-nosed bat, which had long been thought to be extinct, began to make nervous appearances in a tropical rainforest . . . An impenetrable jungle was greener than it had been in decades.

Gloria Delmonico noticed more butterflies in the garden, where there had been hardly any the year before.

Although only polar bears were aware of it, the rate of melt of the polar ice caps slowed.

Temperature gauges stopped going up. Began, ever so slowly, to inch down.

The dreadful pain in Nell Reece's chest eased. She spent less time in bed, getting up earlier in the morning and retiring later. She had not returned to a normal schedule, but one afternoon she inspected the contents of her closet to see if she needed any new clothes. After trying on most of her wardrobe she concluded she would have to throw everything away and buy one size smaller.

The discovery buoyed her tremendously.

The following morning she said, "Jack, I think that awful-tasting medicine is finally beginning to do me some good."

"It's about time. For months I've been thinking that so-called doctor of yours was practicing under false pretenses."

"Doctor Peters has been doing his best; at least I haven't gotten any worse. There was a time when I really thought I would die."

"I wouldn't let you."

She smiled at him. "You would stand at death's door and turn him back, would you? My hero."

"Don't laugh at me, Nell. I mean it."

"The air really is softer. There's been a change in it; subtle, but a change."

"I can tell that too," Jess said from the doorway of the bedroom. "Mom, Jack, can I talk to you a minute?"

"Sure, honey, what is it?"

"More good news. At least I think it's good news; I hope you will too. I'm going to get married."

Nell sat upright in bed. "Don't tell me you've agreed to go to Mars with Evan after all!"

"Not Evan. I'm going to marry Kirby Delmonico."

Nell's eyes blazed. "How dare that freak have the nerve to ask you to . . ."

"He's not a freak and he didn't ask me; I asked him. He refused until after he's had the surgery. He said I had to know what I'd be getting." Jess laughed. "As if I don't know already. I'll be marrying the gentlest, smartest man on Earth or any other planet."

Nell repeated, "*You* asked *Kirby*?"

"I'll take him with or without the surgery," Jess said resolutely. "I never thought I'd be so lucky."

"Jack, you have to talk to her!"

"Why me? She's your daughter; if they love one another it's their own business."

"But . . ."

"Kirby's disfigurement isn't genetic, Nell; their children won't inherit it. But if they inherit their father's brains, the human species may take a leap forward."

"That isn't how evolution works, Jack."

"It's exactly how it works. An unusual random gene appears in the gene pool, and presto! Did Evan tell you about Morgan horses?"

"What do horses have to do with it?"

"A couple of centuries ago," Jack said, "there was a remarkable stallion in the state of Vermont. He wasn't very big but he was beautiful and strong and incredibly versatile. He could pull a plow all day and win races against the fastest horses in the county that same evening. When he was bred to mares of any type the foals they produced were exact copies of their sire. His 'random gene' bred true every time, a unique ability that made him famous. The man who owned him was a farmer named Justin Morgan, so people got to calling the stallion's offspring Morgans. A whole breed developed from them; for a while they were the most popular saddle horses in the States. Evan's mare, Rocket, is a cross between a Morgan and a Thoroughbred. He chose her for that reason and he's very proud of her; she inherited the best qualities of both."

Nell accused, "You're comparing my daughter's having children to breeding horses."

Jess merely laughed. "I like that story, Jack. Is it true?"

"You can look it up in one of Edgar's encyclopedias, that's how true it is."

"If Evan loves his horses so much, I don't know how he can stand to leave them and go to Mars."

"I didn't ask him but I can make an educated guess. Evan's a pragmatic young man; a horse can live for thirty years at the most and Rocket's twelve now. Mars is Evan's future. But when he goes, he's leaving her and Comet with you."

"He can't do that!" Jess protested.

"Of course he can, he owns them both. Evan saved money for years to buy Rocket and have her bred to a good stallion."

"He's trying to make me feel guilty."

"Evan's not like that, Jess; he genuinely wants to give you his dearest possessions."

"Why would he breed horses in the first place if he wanted all along to go to Mars?"

Before Jack could reply Nell said gently, "Sometimes one dream overtakes another."

Lila Ragland was increasingly restless. Her love affair with Shay Mulligan was physically satisfying but did not engage her sufficiently. Lila had always needed a challenge and Shay did not offer one. He was the personification of laid-back, with everything on the surface. What you saw was what you got. Jack Reece, thought Lila, was like an onion, with layers and layers that could be peeled away to reveal new layers beneath.

When Shay told her about Bea's offer of enough money to go to Mars, Lila's reply was immediate. "You jumped at the chance, I hope."

"I most certainly did not, Lila; I'm not that adventurous. Besides, what could I contribute to Mars Settlement?"

"You could be a vet; they're going to have livestock eventually."

Shay shook his head. "Too late for me. By the time the first shipload of colonists blasts off I'll be past fifty, and that's the cutoff age."

"I'm younger than you are," she reminded him. "I could still go."

"Are you serious? A single woman alone on Mars? There's going to be a preponderance of men up there, it'll be like the Old West all over again."

"How *interesting*," said Lila Ragland.

Day by day, planetary temperatures were returning to normal. Mars began to seem less like an escape from the heat than an adventure for the brave. There were plenty of adventurers dreaming of a life on the Red Planet.

Bea was taken aback by Lila's request. Edgar was right, she told herself. They do come out of the woodwork. Her lips drew together like tightened purse strings. "I'm not a lending agency, Lila. You inherited something from Edgar, use that."

"I've spent it. But you offered Shay . . ."

"That was different."

"I don't see how."

"He wanted the money for Evan's dream."

"Well, maybe I want this for my dream."

Bea gave Lila a probing look. "When did you dream about emigrating to Mars? I wouldn't think that was your sort of life.

Besides, I happen to know that Shay's planning to propose to you. It's time he got married again, he's such a domesticated sort of man."

A barely perceptible shudder ran across Lila's shoulders. "He hasn't proposed, Bea. And if he did I'd refuse him."

"He's a wonderful person."

"I'm sure he is. He's just not right for me."

Looking into those green eyes, Bea had a disturbing premonition. "Who would be right for you? Jack, perhaps?"

Long eyelids dropped over Lila's eyes, concealing her thoughts—but not before Bea saw them. "Jack's married to Nell," Lila said coolly.

And you wouldn't let a little thing like that stop you, Bea thought to herself. I'll bet I know what you spent Edgar's money on. Beauty treatments and sexy lingerie.

The big manila folder wasn't bulging anymore. NEST EGG and EMERGENCY had been seriously diminished and would be totally wiped out if employed to protect Jack's marriage. A fund-raiser to augment the money for the hospital was a distinct possibility.

The only value money has, Bea told herself, is the good it can do. Perhaps I've been too cavalier with what Edgar left; as a bank executive I should have known better. But when it comes too easily it can go just as fast.

I'd better arrange for Kirby's surgery before something else turns up.

Bea summoned Kirby to her room. "Do you still want to have plastic surgery?" she asked.

He gave a bark of laughter. "Do I still want to keep breathing?"

"You've talked with Jess about marrying?"

"Only when I cease to be a monster."

The simple courage with which Kirby spoke those words touched Bea's heart. "Then I think we should get started right away," she said. "I understand there will be several operations on your face first, and then later on your hands. You'll be looking at months in and out of hospital and an awful lot of pain; you do realize that?"

He did not blink. "Can we go to the doctor tomorrow?"

24

"It's been a long time coming," Gloria complained to Gerry. "There were times when it seemed like deliberate cruelty, making Kirby wait like this."

"We've been busy going from one crisis to another," he reminded her.

"That's what life is," she said. "Peaks and chasms. You find a peaceful meadow and expect to stay there forever, but five minutes later you're caught in an avalanche. If Kirby has his surgeries, and if they're successful, and if he marries Jess . . . then Sandy will probably get kicked out of the navy or Buster will fall in love with a kleptomaniac or one of the twins will . . ."

"Stop, Muffin! If you'd said all of that years ago I'd have refused to go along with the adoptions."

"And look at all the fun we'd have missed. Lives aren't designed to order, Gerry. They just happen. Like the weather."

"There are some things no one can fix," her husband replied. "How many scientists are trying to make it rain?"

"Is that one of those trick questions, like how many angels can dance on the head of a pin?"

"When the temperature began to go down I really thought we'd have rain too," Gerry said. "But no luck. Clouds form, the sky darkens . . . then the clouds blow away and the sun blazes out again."

"There'll be rain sooner or later."

Gerry put an arm around his wife. "You really believe that, do you?"

She tilted her head back and smiled up at him. "I really do," she said. "I have faith."

The first stage of Kirby's surgeries would be performed at Madison General Hospital. Kirby and Gloria had a consultation with the surgeon several days beforehand. Doctor Gretski was a short, balding man with a top-heavy torso and powerful chest and arms. "Don't let the term 'plastic surgeon' mislead you," he began cheerfully. "There's no plastic involved, in this case the word simply means capable of being molded. I'm a reconstructive surgeon, I re-mold severely traumatized faces.

"There have been some near-miraculous advances in my field. Using laser surgery and surgical glue instead of stitches, we've almost eliminated scarring and reduced recovery time by half. I'm able to give my patients a whole new face if necessary.

"When it's time to do your hands you'll go to someone else; the hand is a specialty by itself. The work has to be done under a high-powered microscope to get the delicate nerves right and rejoin the minute blood vessels.

"Your new face will have total mobility of expression. There will be no numb areas; lips, eyelids—the underlying muscles will move just as they did before the accident. Since the damage to your face is limited to the left side we still have the right side to use as a model to follow, so we'll work from a series of photographs.

"For the rhytidectomy we'll peel off your entire face, reshape the fat, muscle, cartilage and skin, then put it back on. We'll be building a complete new eye socket for you, too. There is a non-absorbable surgical putty that will replace bone structure; it's rather like using Play-Doh."

Gloria, who had been sitting beside Kirby in the surgeon's office, abruptly stood up and left the room.

Gretski's eyes twinkled. "At least she didn't faint; some people do. You're going to look a lot worse before you look better, Kirby, but then you're going to look a *lot* better."

When they got home Flub and Dub pleaded to hear the grisly details. "You should have taken us with you," Dub said, sounding aggrieved. "We wanted to see the surgical ward."

Gloria told them, "We didn't go to the surgical ward, we were in the doctor's consulting room."

"Shit," said Flub.

"You two are grown-ups now," Bea reminded them. "When are you going to start acting like it? You remind me of children at Halloween."

They were not insulted; it was almost impossible to insult either of the twins. They were only sensitive to each other's feelings. "Can we go with you when Kirby's admitted?"

Everyone had the same request except for Nell, who did

not feel up to the long drive yet. Jack would take Kirby, Jess, Bea and Gloria in his car. To accommodate the other inhabitants of Tilbury Farm extra automobiles had to be hired from the rental agency. "Are all these folks part of your family?" the bemused rental agent asked Jack.

"Every one of them."

"Even this pretty girl?" the man inquired, winking at Jess.

"She's spoken for," Kirby snarled, stepping forward to make sure the rental agent got a good look at his face.

"Hey, wait a minute, I didn't mean . . ."

"You bet your life you didn't," Kirby interrupted. "You bet your *life*. Are you prepared to lose it?" Accompanied by a faint hiss, the menace in his voice was unmistakable.

As they were driving away Kirby said with satisfaction, "You know, having a face like this isn't all bad."

When they pulled into the hospital parking lot Gloria noticed that Kirby's clawlike fists were clenched in his lap. "You're going to be just fine," she assured him.

"I'm not worried about the surgery. I only wish the whole crowd hadn't come with us; it's like a circus parade."

"They're here to give you support, Kirby."

"I'm better at coping on my own." The car had barely stopped before he was out of it and striding toward the front entrance. Gloria took his overnight case from the trunk of the car and hurried after him. When he reached the front door she turned around and motioned the others to go back. "He wants to be alone," she mimed several times.

Evan ignored the request. While Kirby was at the admittance desk Evan caught up with him. "What's your problem?" Kirby snapped. He was finding it hard to maintain the cool exterior he wanted.

"No problem," Evan told him, "I just wanted to wish you good luck. I really mean it, Kirby." He gave the other man a light punch on the arm and walked back to the car.

Bea observed Madison General Hospital with a professional interest. The corridors did not seem to be well lit and were hardly wide enough for two wheelchairs going in opposite directions. There were not enough benches for people of a certain age who felt a need to sit down, nor was there adequate signage. Without her spectacles she would not have found the restroom signs. Worst of all, the hospital smelled like a hospital.

Surely something could be done about that!

Edgar Tilbury Memorial is going to be different, Bea promised herself. Taking a small notebook from her handbag, she began to make a list.

Jess stayed with Kirby until the nurse asked her to leave. "Mister Delmonico has to get some rest, he has surgery tomorrow." She waited by the doorway to make sure the visitor left.

"I hope you're going to be pleased with the results of this," Kirby said to Jess when he kissed her good-bye. A careful half kiss, well-practiced.

"You don't have to do it for my sake."

"I'm not; not entirely. I'm doing it for mine. After all these years I'm curious to know what I really look like without the scars."

"You heard what the doctor said, you're going to be very handsome."

"As handsome as Evan?" he asked—though he hated himself for asking.

"It isn't a competition."

"When a man's in love with a beautiful woman he's in competition with every other man."

"That's mega maize, Kirby."

"I'm a mega maize kind of guy," he replied. His gaze followed her through the doorway and down the hall.

"Does anyone ever die under anesthesia?" he asked the nurse.

"Not in this day and age."

"Not ever?"

"Well . . . only if they're seriously ill anyway and have a bad heart."

Kirby gave a crooked smile. "My heart's just fine; the girl who just left here carries it with her everywhere."

As they were driving home from the hospital Gloria was very quiet. She did not make casual conversation, merely stared out the car window. At last Gerry said, "There won't be any problem,

Muffin. It's not a major operation, only plastic surgery on his face, and he's a strong young man."

"Don't dismiss it so lightly. I was given an exact description of the procedure, Gerry, and it scared me to death. Kirby may look like it but he's not a strong young man. The explosion at RobBenn almost killed him; he was the most badly injured of the boys and spent weeks in the hospital."

"That was fourteen years ago," he reminded her, "and he made a full recovery. They just checked him out very thoroughly pre-op, remember? You're not usually such a worrywart."

"Kirby's had bad luck all his life. Falling in love with the same girl Evan loves is another example of it. I don't want anything else to go wrong for him."

"Jess has chosen him, not Evan," Gerry reminded her. "Kirby's about to look like himself again and Evan Mulligan will go to Mars. Relax and enjoy the future."

Gloria gave an embarrassed laugh. "I do get carried away, don't I? Sometimes I forget to count our blessings."

That night the rain came. Like the quality of mercy it fell upon the parched earth. Gloria heard it first, awakened from a fitful sleep by the sound of gentle tapping. She sat up in bed. "Gerry? Gerry, do you hear that?"

The lump beneath the bedclothes stirred. "Wha-?"

"Rain. It's raining!"

He pushed the covers aside and listened. "I'll be damned, so it is. Sounds like we mended the roof just in time."

"I'm sorry you did." She stretched her arms wide. "I'd love to have that sweet, sweet rain come in here with us."

The gentle tapping became a thunderous pounding as the storm gathered force.

Gloria lay back down and snuggled against Gerry. Together they enjoyed a natural music they had not heard for a long time.

In the morning the air was washed as clean as the earth.

Kirby made it clear that he did not want the whole tribe camping in the hospital during his operation, which was scheduled for nine in the morning. "All of you wait at home!" he insisted.

Gloria began telephoning the hospital at nine thirty.

By noon the nurse at the intensive care desk in the surgical ward recognized her voice as soon as she said hello. "You mustn't worry," the nurse said, "this is a long operation. Didn't the doctor explain it to you?"

Gloria telephoned twice more before three o'clock, when the nurse was relieved to be able to say, "They just brought him back from surgery and he's doing well."

"Is he awake yet?"

"Oh no, he'll sleep straight through until tomorrow morning. Do you want us to call you then?"

When the shift changed the new nurse was informed, "You'd better telephone Kirby Delmonico's mother this evening to let her know he's all right."

"That isn't part of the protocol," the other woman objected.

"I know, but trust me. If she doesn't hear from us by then, that woman will break down a door to see him. She's like a mother tiger with one cub."

25

The global climate began to change at an unprecedented rate. From Boston to Bolivia to Bulgaria the extreme weather was normalizing. Environmentalists who had been monitoring the melting of polar ice discovered that it was inexplicably reforming. The oceans cooled rapidly; hurricanes and typhoons diminished commensurately. Marine life that had been on the verge of extinction in overheated seas recovered.

Panels of scientists and meteorologists were assembled to discuss and debate what was happening, but the explanations were as various as the explainers. The West implied the change was a result of their efforts; the East insisted it was to their credit. Neither could prove it.

Doctor Peters took off his stethoscope and shook his head. "I can't explain it, Nell, but your lungs and throat are perfectly healthy. Whatever you were suffering from has cleared up completely. It was highly resistant to medication; I'd begun to fear we were looking at a chronic condition that might plague you for the rest of your life. I have a few other patients with the same problem and they're well now too.

"In this day and age we don't get many mystery illnesses and fewer mystery cures. Wish to God I understood this; it might reoccur sometime."

When Nell told Jack he smiled. "I've always known you were unusual. Now I've got a doctor's word for it."

"It's not me that's unusual, it was my illness."

"It's good for the medical profession," said Jack, still smiling, "to be forced to admit they don't know everything."

The first time Gloria and Gerry visited Kirby in the hospital she told him, "If you weren't all wrapped up in bandages I'd give you a big hug, you clever man."

With his voice muffled by cotton and gauze, he struggled to ask, "*Wha di do?*"

"Your theory about the planet must be right; it looks like Earth's forgiven us. When the military forces began destroying their nuclear arsenals Earth modified the weather."

Kirby looked toward Gerry. "*Dat ri?*"

He looked skeptical. "Gloria thinks it is, but it's not a story I'd take to the papers. It's true there's been an improvement in the global weather, and the ratio of atmospheric gases is back to normal. Exactly *why* . . . well, that's being argued the way the Change was argued. Lots of opinions and no proof."

"I know what I know," said Gloria.

Gerry put an arm around his wife's shoulders and gave her a fond squeeze. "You believe in fairy tales and I wouldn't change you for the world, Muffin, but we have to be logical. The planet's not sentient; it couldn't be. It's just a ball of rock and water."

"Scientists claim there's more invisible dark space and dark matter in the universe than anything else, and you believe them," she retorted. "Why don't you believe me?"

Doctor Gretski proved to be as good as his word. Kirby's recovery time was shorter than he had expected. When the last bandages came off the young man looked at himself in the mirror with disbelief. "I didn't expect this."

Gretski said anxiously, "What's wrong? I hope you're not disappointed."

"You must be joking. What you've done . . . is astonishing. If it weren't for the explosion I would never have looked like this."

"You would have looked very much like this. The left side of your face is now a replication of the right side. Not a duplicate because no one's face is exactly symmetrical, but yours is pretty close. All that remains is for your eyelashes to grow back, and they will. I'm giving you a special liquid to apply to the roots every night. You can get on with your life now, I'm not going to need to see you again."

The garden on the farm had never been so productive. The ground under the fruit trees was littered with apples and pears;

row after row of vegetables awaited picking. "Everything's ripening at once," Bea complained. "It's not supposed to do that." She asked Evan and Kirby to collect the superabundance before it rotted. "We can use the coolest tunnels as a root cellar," she told them.

Side by side, the two men were gathering the harvest. Evan straightened up with a large cabbage in either hand and turned to Kirby. "What did you just say? I didn't quite hear you."

"Will you be my best man at the wedding?"

Evan tossed the cabbages into a basket. "Are you joking?"

"I wouldn't joke about that."

"Be honest, Kirby; we're not friends and probably never will be. Wouldn't you rather have one of your brothers stand up with you? Buster, maybe?"

Kirby shook his head. "None of them are going to Mars."

"What does that have to do with it?"

"That's such a giant step. I'll never take it but I'd like to have a connection with someone who does. To be able to say, 'My best man's in Mars Settlement.'"

Evan laughed. "You want fame at one remove."

"Two removes would be more accurate but yeah, I do."

"I'm sorry I'm going to be so far away, Kirby. I'm beginning to think we might be friends after all."

Leon Sparks was surprised when Bea Tilbury gave him a wedding invitation. He had continued to drop in on her from time to time, though there was never any news about the murder of the Chalmers brothers. That crime had long since gone into the cold case file.

Sparks read the engraved invitation aloud. "Jessamyn Bennett. And Kirby Delmonico . . ." He gave Bea an incredulous look. "Isn't that the disfigured guy? Does this mean she's marrying *him*? How could she?"

Bea smiled. "I do hope you'll attend the wedding; you're in for quite a surprise."

"I just had one."

Nell was sitting at the little French desk in her bedroom, addressing more wedding invitations. "I'm dubious about inviting Evan," she told Jack. "Jess insists on it, but I'm afraid it will be like rubbing salt in an open wound."

"It'll hurt more if he's not invited."

"I do wish they'd postpone the wedding until after *The Ray Bradbury*'s gone to Mars."

"That would mean waiting longer to marry and they're not going to do that, Nell; not even to spare Evan's feelings. He'll just have to man up."

Nell put down her pen and told Jack, "It hurts me to admit it but I simply don't understand people. Did you ever think so many would want to emigrate to Mars? The space agency's adding flights to accommodate more of them."

Jack said, "The agency isn't being accommodating; no

government agency is ever accommodating. They're eager to get their hands on more of the colonists' money. The economics underlying Mars Settlement are probably pretty shaky—not that the government wants that to get out. I predict at least half of those brave settlers will come back to Earth within a year."

"How do you know?"

"They signed up before our climate began to improve, that's how. The climate on Mars leaves a lot to be desired, even for people who don't mind extremes of hot and cold and a lot of blowing dust. Once the novelty wears off and their eyes get hungry for green hills, they'll have the comfort of knowing Earth will be waiting for them, as beautiful as ever. They'll be mighty glad to see it again."

"Evan won't come back," said Nell, "and I don't think Lila will either. On Mars she's going to be like a kitten in a field of catnip."

He raised an eyebrow. "You didn't tell me Lila was going."

"Didn't I?" Nell gave Jack her best deer-caught-in-the-headlights look. "Bea mentioned it, but it must have slipped my mind."

Shay had not been told either. Lila thought of him as her fallback position. If something happened and she did not go to Mars, Shay would be there for her. Lila always liked to have a fallback position. For that reason she decided not to tell him her plans.

She filled out the application forms and took the first medical test; there would be another and more rigorous one shortly before departure, when she would be tattooed with her vital information. The money Bea had given her was safely tucked in the bank, collecting interest, to be doled out as requested. Very few prospective colonists were in a position to make all their payments up front anyway.

At night Lila went outside and gazed up at the sky. She knew exactly how to locate Mars. In the dark, in the quiet, she stared at the Red Planet and mentally traced the twisted trajectory that had brought her to this unexpected future.

She felt as if her soul were too big to contain within her body.

Once Bea came out to stand beside her. "You're really going to go?"

"I really am."

"In some ways I admire you, Lila."

"What do you mean by that?"

"Edgar told me some of your history. Don't worry, I'm sure he didn't break any confidences, but I know you had a rough time in the beginning and you've come a long way against the odds. This will be a fresh start for you."

"My last fresh start," Lila stressed. "I can't do it again."

"That's what I thought until I met Edgar. Don't ever close the door on possibilities, Lila. Something amazing may be waiting for you."

Since sending in his initial application for Mars Settlement, Evan had received a near-constant stream of communications from the space agency. Hardly a week went by without further information or instructions. He had himself weighed and his weight certified by an approved doctor; thereafter he could not gain another pound before departure, though there was no objection to his losing. He was advised as to what he could bring and those items must be weighed and certified too.

On the wall of his room Evan had a calendar illustrated with color photographs of horses. Gleaming show horses, proud stallions, mares with leggy foals who had big wondering eyes. On the calendar Evan crossed out every day that passed, taking him that much nearer to Mars. He tried not to look at the horses. They reminded him of what he was abandoning—no, not abandoning. He comforted himself with the knowledge that both Jess and Kirby loved animals. Rocket and Comet would be starting a new life with them while he was starting one for himself.

He planned to give Jess their gift-wrapped registration papers with her name as the new owner; a sumptuous wedding present.

Whenever Jess looked at the horses she would be reminded of him.

Jess and Kirby were going to be married in June at Tilbury Farm. "Everything is so green now, budded and blossoming," Jess enthused. "It's as if nature's casting a blessing over us."

At Gloria's suggestion the ceremony would be performed by the priest who had baptized the two Delmonico toddlers.

"Does this mean we'll have to start going to his church?" Kirby asked Gloria.

"Only if you want to, it's not mandatory."

"A lot of people have abandoned the habit, but you and Gerry are churchgoers and it hasn't done you any harm."

"It was a choice we made together, Kirby; we felt it was important to add a spiritual dimension to our lives. Faith is the belief in things unseen, like dark space and dark matter."

"And the sentience of a planet?"

"That's another example," she agreed.

"I can never prove it."

"You don't have to prove it, not to me. When I walk barefoot on the grass I'm aware there is life beneath my feet."

"A living entity?" he prompted.

"I never put it into words until I heard your theory," said Gloria. "But on some level I always knew. Thinking about the awful things we've done to this planet makes my heart ache."

"With denuclearization we've stopped at least one form of torture," Kirby told her. "Do you suppose . . . or is it only coincidence?"

"What?"

"That's when the climate started to improve."

———

The wedding ceremony took place on the lawn in front of the house. The guest list read like a Who's Who of Sycamore River, though some of the prominent residents of the town had not survived the war. Instead of wedding presents the guests were requested to make a donation to the Edgar Tilbury Memorial Hospital building fund. Lila had made the suggestion. "People will feel obligated to give more than they would have spent on a toaster."

The wedding day dawned clear and cool. Jessamyn Bennett had not slept the night before but she felt wonderful. Her wedding dress was on the back of the door. At Nell's insistence it was bridal white. Jess had been scornful—"I'm not virginal!"—but when she saw it hanging there, waiting for her, she was glad she had given in.

Nell helped her get ready, doing her makeup and arranging her curls into an elegant coronet. Before Jess slipped on the dress she opened one of the casement windows and leaned on the sill, looking down at the marquee with its rows of folding chairs. "I want to remember every detail of this day," she told her mother.

"You won't; memory's a funny thing. As time goes by there will only be selected highlights, perhaps not even the ones you would prefer."

"Do you remember much about marrying my father?"

"I don't remember Robert Bennett at all," Nell said through tight lips.

––––––

Leon Sparks arrived early. He was disappointed that he could not give Jess a traditional wedding present; in his pocket was a check made out to the hospital building fund for more money than he could really afford. The Delmonico twins were acting as ushers; they inspected his wedding invitation as if they thought he might have forged it. "Do you want to sit on the bride's side, or the groom's?"

Recalling Kirby as he had last seen him, Sparks said, "The bride's, of course."

The air was perfumed by thousands of flowers. Pots and tubs and bowls of blooms had been placed on every available surface. He sat down on an uncomfortable folding chair and waited. And waited. The rows of chairs filled up. A few people with allergies began sneezing.

At last two men came down the aisle and took their places at the front. Sparks recognized one of them as Evan Mulligan, who had been introduced to him by Bea Tilbury. The other was a total stranger; a tall, exceptionally good-looking man who kept turning to look for the bride.

When Jess appeared there was a murmur of approbation. Gowned in white satin with a sheer veil, she was the personification of bridal beauty as she paced up the aisle on Jack's arm. Her face was radiant when he surrendered her to the handsome man who could not possibly be Kirby Delmonico.

But he was.

Leon Sparks stared at him throughout the ceremony, wondering how many other people were as astonished as he was.

The reception following the ceremony spread out from the house and marquee. Guests wandered about on the lawn; a lawn where tiny green shoots were beginning to appear through the drought-stricken grass. The bride and groom were photographed cutting a magnificent white cake and feeding bites to each other. Leon Sparks got in the line to kiss Jess's cheek, but what he really wanted was to have a close-up look at Kirby's face.

There were very few scars; only minute lines that might have been the result of careless shaving.

Kirby caught him looking at them. "Well? Am I good enough for her?"

Sparks was embarrassed. "I don't . . . I mean . . ."

The other man gave a good-natured laugh. "It's okay. Everybody here has managed to sneak a look and I don't blame them, let them satisfy their curiosity. Once today ends the past will be really over and we can start to forget it. Like going to Mars; a new beginning."

Evan Mulligan had dutifully crossed off each of the diminishing days on his calendar. When a courier delivered the latest letter from the space agency he ripped the envelope open with nervous fingers, afraid they were going to tell him there had been a mistake and he wasn't going to Mars after all.

He devoured the words on the single sheet with his eyes, then read from the beginning again. Slowly.

Dear Evan Mulligan,

Please present yourself in front of your state capitol building at ten o'clock on the morning of July 15. The special bus collecting colonists from your area will be waiting there for one hour only. Do not be late. Have your stamped identity documents ready for examination. Do not bring more than the previously weighed and approved luggage. Any excess will be left behind. Say your good-byes before you board the bus. In order to avoid disruptive public scenes you cannot bring anyone with you to the launch site.

Welcome to Mars, Mr. Mulligan

Evan read the letter twice. Welcome to Mars, Mr. Mulligan.

He felt a sudden hollowness in his stomach; a feeling compounded of joy and excitement and . . . and fear, go ahead and say it. Fear. He was standing on the threshold of space, about to step off the edge of the world.

Alone.

The word took on a whole new meaning.

Until he boarded *The Ray Bradbury* and the airlock doors closed behind him he could change his mind and turn back. But how could he face the people he knew if he did that?

How could he face himself?

Evan carefully refolded the letter along its creases and slipped it back into the envelope.

Colonists from your area. Fellow terrestrials. He had never identified himself as a terrestrial before.

I'll be leaving my home *planet,* he realized. My *home* planet.

An almost tactile sense of Earth swept over him. Snow-crowned mountains and fragrant forests, sparkling lakes and mighty seas. The generous planet that had endured terrible abuse and yet offered a bounteous home for mankind.

Leaving seemed like a betrayal.

Evan took a long look at the calendar on his wall. Three more days until departure. There was still time . . .

Mars was waiting.

But Mars was not as beautiful as Earth.

No place would ever be as beautiful as Earth.

Before the rocket had traveled more than half the distance to Mars, the largest thermonuclear bomb ever built was exploded on the planet left behind.

Mortally wounded, Earth screamed with a voice no one had ever heard before.

And began to break apart.